Isadora Stone
and
The Magic Portal

Laura Anne
Whitworth

Cover Artwork by Gemma Louise Banks

This book was written 'In between'

In between asleep and awake.
In between getting the kids in the bath and then to bed.
In between cooking the tea and then serving it up.
In between feeding the baby in the middle of the night
and drifting back into a fitful, caffeine induced sleep.
In between loading the washing and folding it.
In between dropping the toddler off at nursery and
then picking her back up again.
In between the bath running and me getting in it
(very rare!)
In between rocking my crying, teething baby and
finally putting her down to sleep.
The tiredness was all consuming. Never ending.
No matter how hard life may seem, there is always
an 'In between' and you can accomplish great things.
If you put your mind to it, in the in between.
I had a story to tell and I was determined to tell it.
I'd like to thank the following people, without whom,
there would have been no In between.
My long suffering husband.
Without you, none of all of my greatest achievements
would have been possible.
The greatest of all being our incredible family.
You are my rock, always.
My incredibly supportive Mum and Dad.
Who filled in for Mummy and Daddy so many times in
order that this book might be written.
I know you don't consider it a chore, but without your
Help this wouldn't have happened.

My two bright shining stars. My daughters.
Mummy wants this world to be a better place for you.
My best work, always.
And I have said it, and so it is done.

Prelude

Imagine the Unimaginable.

Imagine that as you drink your morning coffee or ride the train to work.

As you chat to your colleague about Dancing with the stars or American Idol.

Or wait in line for that lottery ticket.

Imagine that they are here.

That they have always been here.

As you decide what dress to buy and wear to your prom.

As you park your car and go and do a food shop.

As you take the dog for a walk.

They are here, watching, waiting, hoping.

Waiting for the right time to make themselves known.

The right time to say 'Er Hi!, we're here already. Surprise!'

Waiting for us to 'get' that the world in which we know it, is not real.

The 'White World' as they call it.

Where on a daily basis, what makes front page news is some new celebrity who has had a facelift or breast implants.

Or new political infighting about something wholeheartedly irrelevant.

This is not the real world.

This is just a media smokescreen to hide the real issues that are going on here on Planet Earth.

Trivia to keep our attention away from what is really happening around us.

The real planet Earth and real issues.

If we humans knew half of these they would blow our minds.

We would laugh them off as impossible.

That couldn't happen here!

We are so blinkered, so conditioned to follow the
rat race, and the American Dream, that we make the lives of the
people who control our world easy.
Very easy.
They watch patiently.
Hoping that the Human Race will stop competing, fighting and
blowing each other up
Long enough to realise that the Universe is not just about us.
In fact we are a drop in the ocean.
Actually not even a drop. Maybe a grain of sand in what is a huge vast
sprawling Desert Island.
And that there's lots of Desert Islands!
Hoping that soon we will realise that it's not just about how much
money we make, what car we drive or whether we can afford two
vacations a year.
Preferably to Turks and Caicos.
In fact it shouldn't be about money at all.
Money is just something that has been put in place by the people who
control the planet. To control us the people.
Keep us worrying about money.
Keep us earning money.
Keep us spending money.
Keep us losing money.
When we are busy worrying about where the money comes from, we
don't have enough time to realise that we are slaves.
They watch patiently.
Waiting for a time when the light bulb will switch on.
When people will start to stand up and be counted.
When people will not accept the lies and the disinformation any
more.
When people start to realise,
'Hey, this isn't working for me anymore.'

A time when humanity will realise that Earth is a sentient being, and that we are killing her with our plastics and forms of gas producing transport.

Tonnes upon tonnes of needless rubbish.

Why is this OK? And if we carry on in this vein, it won't matter how much money we make or how many vacations we can afford to take a year. If we have nowhere left unspoilt by man to vacation to.

They watch for a change within mankind, a shift, a sign that we are ready for the truth. The truth of why we are here in the first place. The truth of who they are too and the part that they play in our complex history.

Imagine that they have waited for thousands of years for *exactly* the right time to make themselves known.

Imagine that time is now.

5.00am, Las Vegas, Nevada

Robin's incredible dream in which she was a bird and could fly, was rudely awakened by the shrill piercing sound of her phone. To begin with she couldn't separate her dream and the sound of her phone in her mind, and for a while she was a bird whose song sounded like her mobile phone. Eventually sleep slipped away and reality beckoned.

'What! Jeeez, do you know what time it is?' She immediately regretted this and thinking about the hour said, 'Momma...are you ok?'

'It's me.' There was a long pause on the other end of the phone and the person known to Robin exhaled. 'We've done it Robin, we've captured one.'

'What!' Robin felt sick and excited all at the same time. 'You're kidding me?'

'I'm not kidding Robin, I'm staring at it right now.'

Robin swallowed and rubbed her temple feeling a headache coming on.

'Is it alive?'

'It's alive,' said Mike Jones her research partner.

'Are you there now?' Robin said frantically running around trying to find something, anything to put on. She settled on a gravy stained pair of sweatpants and an oversized T shirt which stank of stale sweat from a recent gym session. She didn't care, she needed something QUICK.

'Yes I'm here now. I just said that to you. I'm here on Level 6. I'm staring at it now.' Mike whispered excitedly

'What does it look like? Does it look like we thought? Does it have those feet that we discussed with the different placement of bones to humans. Is it male or female?

Forget it don't tell me. Don't go anywhere' Robin laughed and half shouted, 'I'm on my way!'

Mike laughed as he cancelled the call.

'Yes we are.' He thought.

8.00am The Whitehouse, Washington DC

The President of the United States sat with his Grandchildren eating breakfast. This morning it was toast with jam and Cheerio's.

As the first lady entered the room he couldn't keep his eyes off her. She even managed to look great first thing in a morning. God he loved that woman. She was beautiful inside and out.

'Grandpa,' said his Granddaughter. 'What are you going to be doing today? Are you going to be catching some bad guys?'

The President of the United States laughed. 'No baby, my job really isn't that glamorous you know. Today I'll probably be sat round a large table with lots of my fellow administration, thrashing around a few ideas. Grandpa will probably just be sat in a room talking all day.'

His Grandchildren looked at each other knowingly.

'Really!' The President of the United States laughed. 'My job is way less exciting and dangerous than you think!' he winked.

Their laugher was interrupted by the strange ring of a phone that rarely rang. They had heard it ring maybe a couple of times before and each time their Grandpa had left pretty soon after.

The President of the United States picked up the phone

'Yes – this is The President'. The voice on the other end of the line said 'Mr President. I'm afraid we have a problem'.

Area 51 Nevada

An hour later Robin was flying down the dirt track that leads past the famous post box and on her way to Groom Lake. She sped past all of the cameras set up along the way to vet and deter any visitors. Robins car understandably passed all security checks as this was her place of work. The place where she came to everyday. Day in and day out.

Robin had dedicated her entire life to studying this creature and others like it. She 'knew' they existed but she had never seen one in real life as they were so very elusive. And now they had one? It was almost too much to bare. Well she reminded herself, 'I say I've never seen one, but there was that one time when I was young. I could have sworn I saw one.'

Robin screeched into the huge sprawling complex and just remembered in the nick of time to switch off her lights. Jeez that would have meant a dead battery and a bump later.

She was half running, half skipping to the entrance of the facility when she realised she should try and act a bit more sedate. This was after all not a place where you should be caught running for anything! You could be shot! Or worse, start a mass panic that something had escaped. And she was a respected and revered Scientist after all and Scientists do not run. Not wanting anyone to get the wrong idea and think that she shouldn't be there at all, she slowed her jog down to a brisk walk.

Once at the door to the complex, she managed to pull her security pass out of the hidden pocket in her bag and flash it at the swiper. She then placed her thumb on the cold plastic. The system recognised her as Robin Miller, Lead Scientist in the 'Cosmic Division'.

The door opened and Robin ran down the corridor to the elevators and pushed the button she rarely pushed. Level 6. The automated voice said 'Please look into the retinal scan.' Robin looked into the scanner trying to keep a lid on the amount of excited butterflies that were threatening to escape from her tummy. Could this really be what they had been looking for their whole lives?' The elevator made a beeping noise which meant Robin's retinal scan had been accepted. The robotic voice announced. 'Doors closing, accessing Level 6.' The elevator descended to Level 6 in the blink of an eye, which did not help the sick feeling that was emanating from Robins stomach. She stepped out of the elevator and hot footed it to the next set of security doors adjusting her top as she went. Man she had got ready quickly. Was that gravy?

'Come on already' she screamed in frustration at the process she had to repeat at the next set of doors. Security was tight in this building. But for good reason. Most people didn't know this building existed. And the ones that did, they were the reason that security was tight.

After what seemed like an age, the doors opened and Robin stepped into the light of the dimly lit Hangar.

Robin's eyes adjusted to the light. She caught sight of what she had been dreaming of meeting her whole life. All the saliva dried up in her mouth.

There, sat at a table and eating from what looked like a large pot of Honey, was a Sasquatch.

The Sasquatch was surrounded by the who's who in the Military and science world and Robins research partner Mike Jones sat opposite.

'Hello' Robin beamed smiling at the Sasquatch. The Sasquatch's face split open into a huge toothy grin, and he let out a HUGE belly laugh.

The day Robin had always dreamed of had arrived. What she had spent her whole life working for, was finally here. And it was better than she could ever have dreamed of.

9.00am, Hood River Valley High School, Odell, Oregon

Isadora Stone sat at her desk at school and watched the rain drops drip down the window. This was insufferable. She was so very, very excited. Tonight she was going to see her 'friend'. Her friend that no one knew about. Nobody at all. The bubble of excitement that she felt in her stomach was now aching. It actually hurt. She must remember to pick up the Honey on her way home. Let's hope Momma didn't ask too many questions again.

Isadora's mind moved to her Momma. She had been very ill recently and no one had been able to find out what was wrong with her so far. Isadora was worried sick about her.

'Isadora Stone!' Mr Porter shouted and jolted Isadora out of her depressing thought. 'Would you like to give us the answer to Question number 1?'

Isadora jumped, she'd been so lost in thought worrying about her Momma that she hadn't got a clue what the teacher was talking about. What class was she in? Maths? Her book wasn't even open. She felt the heat of red colour spread across her face.

'Isadora come and see me after school please tonight.' Mr Porter sneered pointedly peering over the top of his weird shaped glasses.

No no **not** detention, not tonight! Isadora felt sick as anger, fear and shame spread through the pit of her stomach. Tonight she had to be on time as tonight she would get to see Chinga again. Isadora placed her head in her hands. Hopefully he would still be there by the time she got there. Or she could just not turn up to see Mr Porter after class and deal with the consequences? She didn't know what to do. Hot angry tears pricked in her eyes. She was so angry with herself for being caught daydreaming by Mr Porter. She didn't need to remind herself that she didn't have many friends at school and

Chinga had become the closest friend that she had. She really looked forward to seeing him. She swallowed down the sadness. Plus it was always a welcome bonus that the Candy he brought her from his planet tasted like heaven. There was nothing on our Earth like it and no human words to describe it. It was just incredible. And now she might not get to taste it again for another couple of weeks. Plus she loved Chinga and the chats that they had together. He understood her like no one else. Sometimes when she'd had a bad day at school and the popular girls had made her life hell again, she'd considered going back with Chinga to his planet and living there with him. She didn't fit in with the other kids at school. They were all preoccupied with boys and reality TV and the Kardashians. Whoever the hell they were? And Isadora just wasn't. She had tried to get excited about the same things that people her age did, but it just did not excite her. For Isadora, she had always felt different to everyone else. She couldn't quite connect or fit in. The only time she felt really happy was when she was either with animals, stargazing, or talking with Chinga. Chinga spoke to her in her head. She had no idea how he did it, but he did. He could talk normally if he wanted to but most of the time when they were together, they would just communicate in this way. Isadora would 'think' what she would want to say and Chinga would hear it. It was pretty cool. But you had to be careful not to let your inner most thoughts be heard too which was always a struggle! She couldn't leave with Chinga though she thought sadly, as she couldn't leave her Momma. She needed her. There was no one else to look after her but Isadora. Isadora once again felt the knots begin to form in her stomach over her Momma. She couldn't lose her too. She just couldn't.

Isadora sighed and opened her Maths book which she just realised was her French book. No wonder Mr Porter was mad at her. She couldn't even remember what class she was in let alone answer the question.

Isadora looked at Question Number 1. This was going to be a long day.

8.15am The White House, Washington

The President of the United States buzzed the call through to his private office. Away from the open ears of his Grandchildren. Those two were smart cookies. They could always tell from his demeanor when something was wrong.

The phone which had rang was a direct, untraceable line to him from his own special 'army'. The Joint Special Operations Command or JSOC for short. They were assigned to protect him, amongst other covert things.

The President of the United States picked up the phone in his office and took a deep breath. Let's hope this wasn't going to be as bad as he suspected.

'OK, I can talk now. What is the problem?' The President sighed. There was so much going on at the moment he couldn't keep up with how many 'issues' the United States of America had on their radar.

The voice on the other end of the line said, 'We have been informed earlier this morning Sir that a team of Scientists who had been trekking out in the Woods in Oregon looking for Sasquatch, have found one Sir.'

Of all the things that the man on phone could have said to him, this was the last thing The President expected. Problems in North Korea, yes. Issues surrounding the Euro? He expected all of that. But Big Foot? Over breakfast?

'Let me check I've got this correct.' The President said rubbing his forehead with his right hand wearily. Two seconds ago I was eating Cheerio's he thought.

'Bigfoot is real? And someone has found one? What does that mean? Do they still have it with them?'

'Yes Sir I believe they have transported it out to Area 51 Sir', the JSOC operative relayed.

Area 51, now there's a thing he thought. He knew some of what went on in that place. But even as sure as he was President, he knew that things were kept from him and what he was told was on a need to know basis. He knew that there were whole factions of the Military and organisations within America which supposedly answered to him, that kept him in the dark as to what was really going on. The FBI, the CIA, the list was endless. And to be honest, he had that much on his plate right now, it was probably best that it was on a need to know basis. And it looked like apparently he needed to know this.

'Ah well thanks for informing me. Keep me up to speed with what happens with the errr Bigfoot.'

'Yes Mr President Sir,' said the voice on the phone and the line went dead.

The President leaned back in his chair and slowly smiled.

'Bigfoot hur? Well I'll be damned.' And he let out a huge laugh shaking his head.

They'll be telling us that aliens exist next! He thought. Although as he laughed, his brain also acknowledged the fact that this actually was the case. He had met with a group of them whilst he had been in office. They were known to us the population at large as 'The Greys.' But he was sure they were called something else in their world. That was an eye opener. Meeting with aliens to discuss the future of the Earth. He smiled to himself. What would the majority of America think if that was on the manifesto? It was so hard to juggle between being The President which the normal world knew and control the 'White World.' Whilst also having a dotted line into 'Dark Operations'. And under the massive umbrella of 'Dark Operations', sat the contentious topic of aliens. The world just was not ready for that yet. And America was far too powerful right now to open up the 'topic' of aliens. Let them argue about the Oil he thought. For now at least. And he set off strolling back to the breakfast table to finish his Cheerio's.

6.30am, Area 51, Nevada

Sitting opposite Mike Jones, on a red plastic chair, was the reason that Robin had chosen the career path she had chosen all those years ago. She was convinced she'd seen one as a little girl, and had spent years trying to convince her family and finally the world. But no one had believed her.

She couldn't quite believe her eyes. But of course she could as she had seen this face, or one very like it, as a child. Mike swiveled round to greet his colleague and friend. 'Robin – meet our newest recruit!'

Robin stared excitedly into the face of the Sasquatch, or what we commonly call 'BigFoot.'

And he/she smiled back again. A huge toothy grin, with yellow stained teeth dripping with Honey. It was massive, at least 10 feet tall and had a face like a monkey but the body of a human. All covered with what looked to be very warm, orangey, chocolate brown fur. And it smelled very sweet and musky. At least I think that's him and not Mike's aftershave mused Robin.

'It smiles?' Robin exclaimed.

'Apparently so!' Laughed Mike.

'Can you understand what we are saying?' Robin said to the magnificently large hairy creature sat in front of her.

Everyone in the room turned to stare at 'Big Foot'.

Big Foot opened its mouth slowly...

Oh my goodness thought Robin it looks like it's going to speak! Don't be stupid she chided herself as soon as the thought entered her head – that would be ridiculous. It's just an animal. But what if?

The Big Foot took in a large breath and slowly spoke the following words, 'Isadora Stone.'

A huge intake of air hissed around the room as everyone simultaneously inhaled in disbelief.

'Shhhh! Isadora Stone?' Repeated Robin. 'What does that mean? Is that your name?' And it's a 'he' Robin thought!

Oh my goodness the Big Foot just spoke squealed Robin internally. Just as Big Foot said in a very low and gravelly voice.

'Get Isadora Stone. I will speak to her and her alone.'

Mike screamed for an aide to come in the room pronto. 'Duane – research all names Isadora Stone within a 50 mile radius and get me a list of their addresses and contact numbers. Now!'

'Yes Sir.' Duane ran out of the room tripping over his own feet as he went.

Mike scratched his head. When they captured this thing they were just happy that they'd finally caught a Sasquatch and could be the ones who went down in history as finally solving the Sasquatch mystery. But hell. This Sasquatch could talk! And he was carrying around a pot of Honey. Curious.

Things had just got a lot more exciting.

The Sasquatch hiccupped. Took in a large intake of air and then burped the loudest burp you could ever imagine.

'She lives in Oregon. You'll find her in school I think. By the time you find her that is.'

'School?' Said everyone in the room at the same time? Everyone was thinking the same thing, this Sasquatch was crazy.

'Yes.' The Sasquatch smacked his lips together with a blissful look on his face.

'She has Maths first thing on a Tuesday morning I think'

All of the world's finest Military men and Scientists looked at each other at the same time. Searching each other's faces for whether anyone knew what the hell was happening. Had they just slipped into another reality?

Mike shouted Duane back. 'Duane find me Isadora Stone, she lives in Oregon and she's school age, and she's probably going to be in a Maths class.'

'Yes Sir,' said Duane looking confused.

'And Duane!' Shouted the huge Sasquatch as he started to run out of the room.

Duane turned around and nervously looked at the Sasquatch.

'Yes….Sir?'

'Bring more Honey. This pot I brought has run out.'

9.15am, Hood River Valley High School, Odell, Oregon.

Isadora was trying really, really hard to get back in Mr Porters good books. Then maybe she wouldn't have to come and see him at the end of the day. Then maybe she'd still get back in time to pick up Honey, cook tea and give medicine to her Momma. AND make it to see Chinga before he left again. He never stayed too long.

Every question that Mr Porter asked the class, Isadora's hand shot up in the air. However Mr Porter was a resentful man and was seemingly purposely avoiding Isadora's gaze now.

When there was a knock on the classroom door.

The Principal of the school Mrs Carter entered. Isadora was just about to look away when she saw that behind Mrs Carter was a very tall, very handsome looking Cowboy. A whisper shot round the room. Who was this man?

He was dressed in Cowboy clothes, but there was something about him that was not 'normal'. Isadora could not quite put her finger on what it was. He was very, very tall. At least 7 foot and had to bend down to get under the door frame and into the room. He had very pale skin, almost white. Which was in contrast to his appearance of a Cowboy. Didn't they spend all day in the sun? He had white blond hair and dazzling blue eyes. He was dressed in head to toe pale denim. And on his feet were the biggest pair of Cowboy boots Isadora had ever seen. However in contrary to his outward appearance, Isadora had a feeling in her gut that this man was no Cowboy. She was mesmerised by him.

Isadora wasn't sure whether she liked the look of this man at all. There was something 'different' about him. He both intrigued and scared her at the same time. He had the appearance of normality, but everything about him felt abnormal.

The atmosphere in the classroom seemed to change instantly and you could almost taste the excitement in the room. Who was this man and who or what did he want?

Suddenly Isadora heard a voice in her head in a deep booming baritone. 'Yes it's you I've come for. Look at me Ma-am.'

Isadora jumped and stared at the tall man who was staring straight back at her. Did that voice come from him? Up until now, Chinga was the only creature who had spoken to her in this way.

The tall man suddenly broke into a beaming smile.

Isadora heard the voice in her head again. 'Just as I thought, you're a telepath. That's why he asked for you. Interesting.'

What? What is this man talking about? What is going on here? Isadora locked eyes with the tall man again. Is he talking to me? He must be. He's in my head! And he's looking right at me!

Isadora's face went red and she stared down at her desk. Don't be silly, he won't mean me. He's probably looking at someone behind me. She also went red as the man was very handsome and he had a way of looking right into her soul. She really hoped that he had not just heard that. The very tall man maintained her gaze and laughed really loud.

The whole classroom jumped.

Mrs Carter the school principal opened her mouth and laughed. A very annoying habit that Mrs Carter had. Every time she started a sentence she laughed first, and after she finished speaking she laughed again. It drove Isadora crazy and most people who met her for that matter.

When Mrs Carter finally finished laughing she squeaked in her shrill voice. 'Mr Porter, might I trouble you for one of your students please?' Mrs Carter finished the sentence with a laugh as usual.

'Certainly, who is it that you need?'

Mrs Carter laughed and then said the words 'Isadora Stone'

Mr Porters head swung round at record speed in Isadora's direction and a huge frown spread across his face. Isadora could literally see him thinking 'I thought as much, she's in trouble again'.

Isadora hesitated, still shocked as to what was unfolding. Swallowing, she stood up and packed her books away. She could feel all eyes in the room on her. As she started to exit the classroom and walk towards the tall man who had not taken his eyes off of her. The whole classroom started to whisper.

'It's probably her Father, no doubt he's weird just like her.' One of the popular girls whispered. The rest of her pack of friends sniggered. Her name was Verity Ashworth. Her Father was a very lucrative businessman in town and very rich. Obviously due to this Verity had an incredible house with both an indoor and an outdoor pool and seemed to be throwing a pool party every weekend. All of which Isadora was never invited to. It seemed that Isadora was never invited to anything. Her 15th birthday back in April had passed much the same as it had always done. No pool parties for her.

Isadora's face went red and she felt heat and anger spread across it. She whipped her head round and stared straight at the girl. How dare she mention her Father. 'It's not my Father!' Isadora snapped her face glowing bright red. 'My Father disappeared a long time ago'.

Verity shrugged her shoulders, 'Who cares.' And the whole pack of girls broke into laughter.

Isadora's heart sank, she missed her Father so much. She felt tears pricking her eyes. Please don't cry now. Not in front of them, she said to herself. They are not worth your tears. She sensed that Verity was jealous of her for some reason. Even though she made out like she thought Isadora was nothing. Isadora could not think of one reason why Verity should be jealous of her.

'Don't listen to the sleepers Ma'am, they are insignificant. You have a higher purpose now, come.' Said the booming voice in Isadora's head. Isadora shivered and looked at the tall man. He was smiling at

Isadora in a kind way and her heart did a little flip flop. Damn he was handsome. The fact that this man was handsome was also not lost on Verity and the rest of the girls. Verity looked at Isadora and then the gorgeous Cowboy. Who is he? And why does he want her? Verity wondered. She was annoyed.

Isadora looked at the tall, handsome man. Did she stay here with Verity Ashworth and her cronies for another 45 minutes of misery? Or did she keep walking forwards and go wherever this man wanted her to go? And what about her meeting with Chinga? She had so wanted to see him tonight. And what about her Momma? She needed to be back in time to give her her medication.

'I am taking you to Chinga.' The voice inside her head said. And don't worry about your Momma, I've fixed her.'

Isadora felt sick, excited and curious all at once. Staring at the tall man, she took a deep breath and walked towards him. Leaving the laughter of Verity Ashworth, her cronies and the misery of the classroom behind.

Mrs Carter laughed.

The Beginning

Nobody spoke as they walked down the corridor. When the tall man became level with the front doors of the school. He turned round and took Mrs Carter's hand.

'Thank you Mrs Carter, it's been a pleasure as always Ma'am.' The Cowboys booming baritone voice rang out and echoed round the high ceilings of the school. Yep, thought Isadora, it's definitely his voice in my head.

'No problem Orion, laughed Mrs Carter. Anything for you'. Orion leant forward, tipped his hat and kissed Mrs Carters hand. Mrs Carter blushed crimson from her toes to her ears.

Orion gestured to Isadora to exit the school. She swallowed and stepped into the bright sunshine of the parking lot. There in the parking lot was a very large, very long black car.

Orion walked to the car and opened the passenger door and beckoned her to jump in. His eyes danced as he sensed her reticence. Isadora took a deep breath and got into the car wondering what the hell she had got herself into. As the car pulled silently away from her school as quiet as a feather humming in the breeze, Isadora swore that she could still hear Mrs Carter laughing.

Orion sat opposite Isadora in the back of the huge black car. His legs were splayed and he was sprawled with the grace of a panther across his side of the car. It was like a limousine inside this car. Isadora was sat opposite Orion. Trying to put as much space between them as possible. He made her nervous. On closer inspection of this large man, he was breathtakingly handsome. We're talking Brad Pitt handsome at the height of his fame. Like 'Meet Jo Black' handsome. He smiled at her obviously knowing what she was thinking. Isadora blushed, again. But whilst he was handsome, there was something in his face that she had never seen before, an unfamiliarity. Yes he made her very nervous.

She looked away, the smell of new leather was overwhelming in this car and Isadora started to feel really sick.

She plucked up the courage to speak. 'Who are you?' She enquired. 'And how do you know Chinga? Is he OK? Why has he sent you to get me?'

The tall man took a deep breath and began.

'My name's Orion Ma'am. I work for the United States Government and I have been sent to bring you to Chinga.'

Orion? That's an unusual name Isadora thought. But then again this guy *was* unusual.

'Bring me to Chinga?' She said. 'Why where is he? Is he OK?'

United States Government? She thought horrified, Oh god what had she got herself into here?

'Do not panic Ma'am,' Orion said with a cat like smile. 'Chinga is currently sat in an underground Hangar in a facility of ours which is known to the public as Area 51. He's asked for you specifically and says he won't talk until you get there. Which is where we are going now'

Area 51? Oh god it gets worse, Isadora gulped. She felt like she could not get enough air. The smell of Orion's aftershave was also making her head spin. Isadora had heard of Area 51. It was where the government were supposed to take any crashed UFO's and it was supposed to be top secret. What the hell was Chinga doing there? Well he is a Sasquatch she thought. Isadora's mind was racing. And that was where they were going? She was going to Area 51? This was not going to be good.

'Why is Chinga there? What are you doing to him? Are you going to let him go? Why are we going there? If we go there are you going to let me go? I have to get back to my Momma. She's ill and I have to look after her. She's all I have and I'm all she has.' Hot tears of sadness spilt out of Isadora's eyes when she thought of her Momma and how much she loved her. She couldn't bare it if anything happened to her because she hadn't got back home in time to give her her medicine. These past few years since Daddy had disappeared had just been too much.

'Relax Isadora, your Momma is fine. Good ol' Orion here's made sure of it. I fixed her up good do you hear?' Orion's voice was like melted chocolate. He sounded like he came from Texas. Isadora thought she could listen to his accent all day.

Isadora didn't understand what he was saying to her about her Momma.

'You've fixed her up good? How can you do that when the doctors don't even know what is wrong with her? If the doctors can't even help her, how can you help her?' Isadora shouted and she turned to look out of the window as a large guttural sob threatened to break out of her chest. Yet she sensed that he was telling her the truth. She could tell that this was a man who did not lie. It was almost as if light shined out of him. She could just tell that he was *good*.

'Your Momma is healed Isadora Stone. You have the word of Orion. And I never lie. No Ma'am I would never do that.' Orion whispered in a low soft voice.

Isadora looked at Orion in stunned silence. She searched his eyes for answers. He looked like he was telling the truth, but how could that be?

'How have you fixed her?' Isadora asked.

'We can't have you worrying about your Momma, when we need you to concentrate on what we need you to do for us now' Orion laughed.

'What do you need me to do for you now? Isadora cried. Have you hurt my Momma? Please, please tell me my Momma is OK?' Isadora sobbed as the emotion broke free from her chest.

'Isadora your Momma is better than OK. She's back to the Momma you once knew and you will see this when you get home. But for now Ma-am. Now we need to deal with Chinga.'

Isadora stared at this man in disbelief. Had he really healed her Momma? Could it be true? She looked into his eyes searchingly and a bubble of hope began to form in her stomach.

'You've really healed my Momma?'

'Yes Isadora, I promise. Here, look!'

Orion handed Isadora something which looked like a clear piece of Perspex. It was light as a feather and as she touched it, little spirals of waves ran out from her fingers like a drop of ink in a pool of water. It looked like heat waves but it was cool to Isadora's touch. It started to mold to Isadora's hand. She jumped and tried to shake it off.

'Relax Isadora and think of your Momma said Orion. And you will see that I'm tellin the truth.'

Isadora blinked away the tears. She wiped her nose with the hand that was unencumbered by this strange Technology and thought about her Momma. Her eyes started to drip with hot stinging tears of sadness and pain. She thought of how kind her Momma was. How much she had suffered when her Daddy had disappeared. How she had wept night after night into her pillow crying out for Oliver Isadora's Father till she had no more tears of pain left. How she had then turned to drinking to ease her pain. Drinking herself into an angry stupor every night. And how eventually she had gotten so ill that even drink did not add any relief anymore. Her Momma had simply given up and was wasting away, staring into space. Isadora had often wondered if she was slowly dying of a broken heart.

As she thought of her Momma. The contraption that she was holding that had molded to her hand, started to shimmer like sunshine on water. Slowly a picture of her Momma became visible. It was playing like a video, but Isadora could tell that it was happening right now. Isadora could not believe her eyes. She looked at Orion and then back at her Momma. Her Momma looked back to normal. The life was back in her eyes and face. Her body was no longer wasted and she had a light rosy colour to her cheeks. She was excitedly cooking tea in the kitchen for Isadora's return from school and singing 'Dancing Queen.' Whilst dipping her finger into a homemade cheese sauce to check the seasoning. Macaroni Cheese. Isadora's favourite. Isadora burst into tears of joy.

'How did you do this?' She cried. 'Thank you Orion so much. How did you heal my Momma?' She almost jumped up to hug him but stopped herself just in time.

Orion smiled, 'You can hug me later,' he winked. 'But for now we need to go and see Chinga.'

Isadora smiled at this weird and wonderful man and wondered how on Earth this guy had healed her Momma? Who was he? What was he? Whatever he was, Isadora thought he was incredible. She blushed again remembering that everything she thought, Orion could hear too.

Orion smiled and took her hand, Isadora gulped and jumped like she had been hit by a bolt of electricity. His hand felt warm and cold all at the same time. 'There are a great many things that you are yet to learn about the Universe Isadora. A great many things. But I believe you are about to become enlightened. I think you may have already guessed, but I am not from this planet. I am from a place called Alpha Centauri. It is a group of stars. I came to your world a long, long time ago. Your world needed help. And since then it seems, your world and your people have always needed help. So I have stayed. I have stayed to help the humans, so you can find your rightful place in the Cosmos.'

Isadora stared at this massive, tall, handsome yet strange man with wonderment. What did he mean? What? The Cosmos? What did that mean? The Universe? Isadora shook her head. How had he healed her Momma? What did he mean he was not of this Earth? She had guessed there were other worlds due to her relationship with Chinga, but the true impact of what that meant had never really reached her. There were other worlds? Other than Chinga's? Wow, that was really awesome. But also quite scary at the same time. She didn't care. She couldn't wait to go home and hug her Momma. Hug her and never let go. And she couldn't wait to taste her Momma's Macaroni Cheese again.

Suddenly the car stopped.

Isadora looked out of the window. She had been so engrossed in her conversation with Orion that she did not notice that they were in the desert. Well it looked like the desert to her. Her surroundings were red barren land. How did they get here so very fast? They'd only been in the car what, 10 minutes? What **was** this car? It wasn't like anything she had ever been in? She suddenly realised that this car was very high tech. Nothing looked normal. How had she not noticed this before?

'Please,' said Orion tipping his hat. 'Let's go and speak to your friend.' And he gestured for Isadora to step out of the car.

Isadora took one more look at her hand which showed her Momma. She was now doing her makeup in front of the mirror, something she had not done for such a very long time. She was rubbing her left eye as she'd accidently poked the mascara wand into it. A bubble of joy danced up Isadora's tummy. She breathed in her Momma and a feeling of intense joy took over her body. Whoever this man was, wherever he was from she *knew* he was telling the truth and her Momma was back to normal. The 'Momma' that she knew and loved before the desperation of her Daddy's disappearance took hold.

Isadora stared at the handsome man in front of her, looked into his eyes and felt that she was finally safe. A feeling she had not felt in a very long time. He looked back at her and smiled. The big beaming smile that he had, which she already recognised. He winked and said 'Better take the Smart Glass Pad back off of you before we go in, if you're finished looking at your Momma? She's fixin up pretty as a picture aint she?'

Isadora realised that he was talking about the thing that was currently molded to her hand. She took one more look at her Momma and then Orion did something with his hand. The small, weird Perspex thing unhooked from her hand and turned into a plain piece of see through plastic once more.

Isadora shivered. What was that thing? She began to realise that nothing was 'normal' when you were with this man.

Isadora looked up at Orion again and he winked.

Her heart did a little flip flop.

She took a deep breath and stepped out of the car.

Area 51

Robin was starting to feel anxious. Where were they?

Duane had left what seemed like an age ago. She was literally sat in front of her childhood dream. The Sasquatch or BigFoot. Whatever you wanted to call it. It was alive, it was here and it was better than expected as he obviously had a fantastic personality. If his huge belly laugh was anything to go by. But she couldn't get him to talk as he would only speak to a schoolkid? Robin sat on her hands. Chinga looked at her again, burped and laughed. 'More Honey' he smiled.

The reason that she had chosen to go into this field from an early age was because of her experience as a child. When she was young, about 3 years old, she had been at a barbeque with her family. She had been playing out in the woods with her cousins at the end of her family's ranch. She had got lost as it had started to get dark. She was scared and couldn't find her way back in the woods. Out of the shadows she had seen what she later believed when she got older to be a 'Bigfoot'. She had at the time been scared to death by this huge hairy creature and had started to run very quickly in the opposite direction. However she quickly saw that the creature was smiling and she sensed that it meant her no harm. That big, furry Sasquatch had held out its hand for Robin to take. And Robin had spent a lovely thirty or so minutes walking with the Sasquatch as it led her safely back to the end of her family's ranch.

She tried to tell her Momma that night what had happened but her Momma thought it was her daughters over active imagination and that there were no such thing as Bigfoot. She dismissed her and told her to go to sleep. This she guessed had driven her into the field she was in. To try and prove that the experience she had experienced as a child was real. That she had seen one. That she wasn't crazy.

Robin stopped reminiscing. Her headache was starting to get worse. She had tried to engage the huge creature in conversation and the only thing that he would tell her is that his name was Chinga.

When Robin had come to work at Area 51, she had been catapulted into a world beyond her wildest dreams. There was certainly never a dull moment that is for sure. In the first few weeks she had been introduced to three different alien civilisations that the American Military were working with. In her first week! Firstly that was crazy in itself. Number 1 that there were even aliens at all and number 2 that the Americans were working with them! They had casually introduced each of them to her like it was just a normal thing! Like Hi! This is an alien and we work with them! Robin had wished that they had explained this to her BEFORE they had just rocked up to her research lab with an Alien being. It had given her the fright of her life.

The first one she met was what we now know as a 'Grey'. Classic big head, huge black eyes and skinny body with skin that had a greyish tinge. The second that they brought had been a being that looked similar to a Grey. It was a lot smaller and had human looking eyes and was really cute and shy. She thought that these beings were referred to as the Oranges. The third she would never forget and still haunted her dreams sometimes. She really hoped that she never saw one of those again. She shuddered thinking about it. It was tall, very tall. Like taller than any human. Robin thought it must have been at least 10 feet tall. It had a humans body but really muscular. Much stronger than any average human and its chest must have been at least three feet wide. It was black in colour with small wings protruding out of its back, but Robin had thought there was no way that those tiny wings could ever have lifted this creature off of the floor. They must have just been for show. But the scariest thing was this creatures head. It had the face of a reptile. With huge yellow eyes with black slits for pupils. When this creature looked at you it had a way of making you feel like it was seeing directly into your soul. The feeling she had felt from this creature when she had been in its presence was pure evil. Like it was the devil itself.

She would never forget that day. She had been working in her lab on some clay casts of what she believed to be Bigfoots feet. One of the Military guys who was very high up there, had shouted her name. She turned around to talk to him and there was this huge monster stood next to him. That's the only word she could use to describe this being. A monster. Robin remembered the smell that emanated from the creature and it made her feel nauseous even now. It was like a weird musky smell. Her encounter with that being had not been a positive one to say the least. She remembered it and shivered. It had wanted her to provide some test results that Robin was working on. It never spoke to her directly. It just got the Military guy who it was with to bark orders at her on its behalf. She couldn't really explain the feelings she had felt in this beings presence other than absolute, abject terror. It had only happened the once and she didn't want it to happen again. Not in this lifetime. Fortunately since then, she had never seen this being again. The other two aliens she had met had been just fine so her overall impression of aliens in general was a pretty good one. Robin laughed to herself and shook her head. What would the average Joe think if they knew all of this was going on underground?

Other than those 3 times where she had personally met live alien beings, she mostly walked past the dead aliens that were preserved in the tall glass Perspex jars every day on floor 3 of her workplace. They were remnants of crashed aliens crafts that were there as a reminder that we weren't the only ones on Earth, or in the Universe. They were put there to keep the scientists going. Keep looking. Keep trying. But she knew that her clearance only allowed her to see so much. There were whispers on the corridors and in the toilets that 'the powers that be' i.e. the people who were really in charge, were in league with some of these aliens. That we were already building bases up in our Solar system and beyond. But Robin didn't know if this was just idle gossip. I mean could we really have left Earth? And if so, what were we doing up there? Robin just thought that was fabrication. Seeing aliens walk around her day after day whilst she was at work was enough right? She put the gossip down to just that. If we'd really left the Earth and were up there with them then that would be crazy, just crazy. However she knew that she did not have top clearance. She had a high level of clearance for sure otherwise she would not be sat in this room now. But she knew that there were people many, many levels higher up than her working at this facility. Therefore undoubtedly, there were many secrets that Robin herself was not aware of.

Robins mind was wandering.

And they were starting to run of Honey.

Suddenly she heard the lock opening on the secure room they were in. The door opened and in walked an absolutely huge man. Robin felt her pulse quicken. She had seen this man around the facility many times but never directly worked with him. They passed like ships in the night and she had never really spoken to him. But I guess you could say she watched him from afar. He made Robin's entire body go warm and fuzzy. She drank him in. He was always dressed in Cowboy clothes. Pale denim, Cowboy hat and huge Cowboy boots. He had a way of looking at you like he was looking inside of you. If he ever made eye contact with Robin when they were in the same space, he made Robin blush. He was *very* handsome. He had intense blue eyes that looked right inside of your soul, and they kind of danced. She believed his name was Orion. Apparently down to toilet gossip with most women who fancied their chances with him, he was an alien from Alpha Centauri. Well a type of humanoid alien. There were so many of the humanoid looking types that were an alien that Robin sometimes couldn't keep track. She didn't really count the ones that looked like humans as aliens. Robin gulped and took in a huge breath of air. She could smell his amazing aftershave. What WAS that aftershave! It made her feel lightheaded. She so wished that she wasn't dressed in a top that was covered in gravy, and pants that smelt of sweat right now.

Orion stepped into the room, tipped his hat and stepped to the side. The light of the outer corridor shone into everyone's eyes and Orion beckoned to someone. The body of a teenage girl stepped into the light. Her silhouette lit up the room. She was fairly tall Robin guessed for her age, and thin, very thin. The girl stepped forward into the light, and was illuminated for all to see. Robin stared at the girl, she looked quite nervous Robin thought. Who is this girl? This willowy, shy looking girl? And why does Chinga know her and want her here? Robin guessed she was around 14 or maybe 15 years old. The first thing that struck Robin was this girl had very old eyes. Eyes that had seen too much, way too young. But never the less her eyes were beautiful. Soulful you might call them. These eyes were on a gangly body and she was obviously dressed in her school uniform. She had beautiful blond hair which was that blond it looked almost white, scraped fiercely back into a ponytail. She was also very pretty Robin thought, although she looked like she had no idea that this was the case. Robin liked this girl instantly. There was something very likeable about her, like you just wanted to sit down and talk to her. This must be Isadora Stone.

'Hi said Robin. I'm Robin Miller, Orion right?' Robin bravely held out her hand to shake Orion's. His hand was firm and both cool and warm all in one. Robin started to feel hot.

'Yes Ma-am, that's me.' The huge Cowboy winked at Robin. 'And as requested, this is Isadora Stone.'

Robin turned to face Isadora, 'Hi Isadora, I'm Robin Miller, I'm a Scientist here at Area 51. I specifically study the Sasquatch amongst other things.' Robin gestured over to Chinga. So far, Orion with his gargantuan maleness had obscured Chinga from Isadora's view. As soon as Robin gestured to Chinga, Orion moved to the side and Isadora saw him.

'Chinga!' She cried and ran over to him. 'Are you OK? Are you hurt? What are you doing here?'

Chinga jumped up and hugged Isadora and a huge smile split over his face. Out boomed his huge infectious belly laugh that Robin had already become used to. 'Isadora, I knew you would come.' They hugged each other tight and it was evident for all to see in that room that Isadora and Chinga loved each other very much.

'OK, now Isadora is here, I am prepared to talk,' the great Sasquatch said to the room. He put Isadora back down out of the huge bear hug that had enveloped her.

All the people that were in the room listened intently and started looking at each other excitedly. The silence was deafening.

Robin swallowed and licked her lips.

'I am here, because I want to be here. I have allowed myself to be caught.'

Robin's eyes darted across to Mike Jones her research partner, they looked at each other knowingly. Allowed himself to be caught? Why would he do that?

The Sasquatch continued, 'There is a reason that the people of Earth have never captured one of us before. Why you can never quite find us. Why you will sometimes find tracks, but still never catch up to us. Why we hide in the shadows and you're not quite sure if you have really seen us or not. The reason we are elusive and you cannot ever find our habitats or track us down, is there are only a few of our kind that still live on Earth to watch over the humans. The rest of us left Earth a long time ago to live on a planet called Delavia.'

A buzz of whispers shot around the room.

I knew it!! Thought Robin!!! I knew there had to be a reason why we'd not tracked them down after all these years! Yet when she replayed what the huge Sasquatch had just said in her head, he had said that they were originally from Earth. And that some of his kind still lived on Earth.

Any other room on the Earth and this statement alone would have caused a huge gasp. Cries of Aliens here on Earth? How can this be? A new planet called Delavia? But not here in this room. In this room everyone here knew of the existence of aliens as they worked with them on a day to day basis. They had for the most part become the 'norm' for the people who were situated in this room currently. Of course not all people at Area 51 knew the extent of the alien lifeforms on planet Earth. Due to the different clearance levels and depending on what area you worked in, depended on what you got to know. Some people working at Area 51 with the lowest levels of clearance just 'thought' that the higher clearance levels might be working with aliens but they were never *really* sure. The people who worked on the upper levels of the facility who had the lowest level of clearance, had to cover their heads with a bag when aliens were arriving and leaving, if they arrived above ground. So they never saw them at all. However it wasn't very often they arrived above ground nowadays. The facility was such that only if you had a certain 'Cosmic Clearance' would you have knowledge of what was really going on in the lower levels of Area 51. All of the lower levels where most of the covert stuff took place, were connected to a huge, superfast, Tram system underground. This Tram system connected out into all of the Underground Bases that were dotted around most of the United States. There were a lot of these Underground bases. Nowadays most of the Aliens that visited Area 51, rocked up on this underground Tram system so nobody without Cosmic Clearance really got to see them anyway.

However, that being said, nobody on Earth up until now had known for certain that the Bigfoot was an alien. Or to describe it more accurately, originated from Earth but many had migrated to another planet. There were suspicions of course. But nothing factual or concrete. Nothing confirmed. Robin knew this to be true now, as the Military bods who were in the room with them and were much higher level security clearance than her, were currently having a fervent conversation between themselves in hushed tones. They were worried.

'Shhhhh please,' cried the Sasquatch to the whispering Military men.

'I have allowed myself to be caught as I need your help.'

Now this statement did make everyone in the room gasp and people started to murmur.

'What do you need our help for?' Asked Robin excitedly. She was thinking that this was possibly the highlight of her career and the best day of her life up to press.

'The Sasquatch as you humans call us, are getting sick.' Chinga said quietly.

Isadora grabbed hold of Chinga's hand 'What do you mean? What is happening?'

'A lot of our kind are really ill, and some of us are dying' said Chinga his normally happy eyes filled with sadness.

'I don't understand,' said Isadora, 'How?'

'Well we've thought about it long and hard. At first it was just a hand full of us getting sick and then more and more of us started to get sick and some of us have died. However the Ancient families in our world have been unaffected. We couldn't understand what it was, until recently and we think we understand now. It is *your* Honey.'

'What?' Said Robin. 'Our Honey?' Robin's brain was working a hundred miles an hour to make sense of what Chinga was saying.

Chinga continued 'The Ancient ones on our planet have always owned their own bees. They came from Earth to Delavia thousands of years ago through the portals on Earth. Some of our kind stayed on Earth to watch over the humans and remind them of their history when the time was right. Others of our kind, seeing the way that humans treated Earth, left to start a new world on Delavia. One of our kind had found Delavia by mistake when they accidently walked into a portal in the woods. Delavia is a paradise. One of the Ancient ones who discovered Delavia came back and told our people about this new world. A decision was made. Some decided to stay as Earth was their home. Others decided to leave, and start a new life on a paradise planet that was unspoilt by humans. Our Ancient ones took some Earth bees with them when they left to colonise Delavia. As our love for Honey is so strong. We cannot resist it. The flowers of Delavia are so sweet and pure and delicious, that their nectar makes the most *incredible* Honey. Over time the Ancient ones got greedy. They wanted all of the Honey that our bees make for themselves. And now the Ancient ones will not share the Honey that the bees make with the rest of us on Delavia, Chinga said sadly. Over the years they have given us Candy which is made from the Honey of their bees when we have done something for them in exchange. And we have all become addicted to the taste. But those of us who don't own our own bees, have to come through the portal to Earth to get a quick Honey fix. It is those of us who travel regularly to your world that have been affected. I too myself am starting to feel sick.'

Why the hell has he just been sat here guzzling the stuff for the past 3 hours if it's killing him? Robin thought. But she politely asked, 'So if it's making you ill, can't you just *not* eat it?'

Chinga smiled wryly. 'How would you feel if I told you not to have your morning coffee? For us Honey is irresistible, we cannot live without it. We are powerless to resist it, and the more we have, the more we want.'

Robin thought about coffee, there was no way she could live without it. If she didn't have at least 3 cups of the stuff in a morning prior to talking to people, she couldn't even communicate. This reminded Robin that she hadn't had any coffee yet that day. She felt a panicky feeling in her chest. 'Why can't you all just take more bees through the portal to Delavia?' Asked Robin irritably. 'Then you could all eat Honey?'

Chinga was looking sadder and sadder, 'The Ancient ones won't permit it. The portals on our world are all heavily guarded to make sure we don't do this. They will allow us to come to Earth and get our Honey fix here, but they won't allow us to bring any more bees back in case they are tainted and they breed with the pure Ancient Delavian bees.'

'Tainted', said Isadora. 'What do you mean?'

'You humans do not keep your world as clean and as beautiful as we do on Delavia'. Chinga explained. 'Delavia is Paradise'.

Mike had been sat stroking his chin and listening intently to everything Chinga had said. He said in an incredulous voice, 'So I'm sorry, you said that the Sasquatch come through a portal to Earth? What do you mean?'

'There are many portals on your Earth where the Sasquatch can come through. You humans do not seem to be aware of this on a wide scale for some reason. Through the years there have been small groups of humans who knew how to access these portals. However through time the secret seems to have died out and the human race is no longer aware that they can travel to other worlds from certain places on Earth. Only at certain times of day and in certain days of the week, not all of the time. In certain places on your Earth when the energy or magnetism is right, a portal will open between Earth and our world. We have always known this on Delavia, as we came from Earth. And when we can come through to Earth, to collect Honey, we do. We come through, find Honey and go back. That is why you have never caught us as we do not stay for long. We come at night where possible and we stay in the shadows and mostly where your people don't go. Those of us who stayed on Earth and who still live here, live deep, deep in the forest. We know where to hide from humans so we won't be found. Not until humans are ready.'

This was true Isadora thought. Isadora snuck out to the woods most nights. It had started when she was young and her Daddy used to take her out there star gazing. Then after he disappeared, she used to go out every night into the woods star gazing, as it made her feel closer to him. Then in more recent times, it was escapism for her to get away from the angry character her Momma seemed to have become when she drank. She went to the woods every night and the only reason that she had seen Chinga was because she had taken Honey sandwiches with her as a snack and the smell had drawn Chinga out. Otherwise they never would have met at all, with Chinga always hiding in the shadows.

Robin and Mike locked eyes again. They had heard rumours about these portals, but this information was above even their clearance level it would seem. Their thought was punctuated by Isadora saying to Chinga 'You said you needed our help? How can we help you?'

Chinga took a deep breath, 'Something is wrong with the Honey that has been brought through from your world to ours recently. It has for a while now not tasted the same. But something now has changed even more and it is making my people sick. We need you to change it back, to make it right again. And we need you to find a cure for our civilisation before we all get sick and die. I need you to come to Delavia and make us all better before it's too late.'

A silence settled around the room as everyone was deep in thought with all of the new information that Chinga had just divulged. Firstly they had just today found out that the Sasquatch was real and now there were portals on the Earth that people or creatures could pass through. And now a Sasquatch was saying that he wanted them to GO to his world. And there was something wrong with our Honey? What did he mean by that? Our Honey was fine, nobody had gotten ill here with it and millions of people ate Honey every day? Most

American foods had Honey in them! If there was something wrong with our Honey there would be millions of people dying all around the Earth right now wouldn't there?

Robin was the first to speak, 'So what do you want us to do?'

Chinga looked at Robin. 'I want you to send a party of your best scientists and doctors to Delavia and figure out what is wrong with us, and I want the rest of your Scientists to stay here and test your Honey and find out what has changed.'

'OK,' said Robin. 'We can do that.' She would do ANYTHING to spend just a bit more time with this Sasquatch and the opportunity to go and visit where he actually lived had just about blown her mind.

Robin looked over at Isadora who was still looking at Chinga with love and concern in her old eyes, and Robin wondered suddenly why the huge Sasquatch had asked specifically for this girl.

What was so special about her? And how did he know her in the first place?

'And why did you ask us to find Isadora Stone, Chinga?' Robin asked the Sasquatch quizzically.

'Isadora has an ability, one which she probably isn't aware of yet. She can talk to our kind not just how you and I are talking now, but she can hear us in her head if we choose to communicate telepathically.'

Isadora's mind was racing, I guess she already knew this as she had heard what she now knew to be Orion in her head back at the school, but she still hadn't figured out what that actually meant? And here was Chinga saying that she could talk to aliens in her head. Why was this? Could other people do it? Was she weird? Of course she was weird she thought sadly, the girls at school reminded her of that every day.

Chinga continued, 'Some of the Ancient ones on our planet have lost the ability to talk normally over the years and we will need someone from your planet to communicate with them telepathically.'

Isadora suddenly could see where this was leading. She felt sick and excited all at the same time. Like electricity was running through her entire body.

Chinga looked at her, 'I want Isadora to come with us.'

2.00pm, The White House, Washington DC

The President had been thinking about 'Bigfoot' for much of the morning. Sure he'd been 'there' in the meetings he'd attended that day. But he'd not really been *there*. It was just a strange thing to suddenly find out that something that you thought was a myth, was actually real. He wondered what it looked like?

Suddenly the private phone in his office rang again and jolted him out of his thoughts. This must be the update he hoped.

'I'm so sorry!' The President explained to the Prime Minister of the United Kingdom. 'Would you excuse me whilst I take this call. It's very important and I have been expecting it.'

'Certainly! Not a problem go right ahead,' said the Prime Minister. 'I will just go and use the facilities.' He left the Oval office with a look of distain on his chubby, red face.

The President picked up the phone.

'This is The President.'

The same monotone and matter of fact voice from earlier began to talk.

'Update on the Sasquatch situation Sir. The Sasquatch is an alien from a planet called Delavia, although it originates from Earth. Some of the Sasquatch still live on Earth but this one that's been caught is one of the ones that lives on the planet Delavia. The Sasquatch on Delavia are getting sick as they are coming through a portal on our Earth to come and eat our Honey. The Sasquatch has requested we send a party of scientists and doctors through the portal Sir, to go and heal the creatures that are sick. He also wants us to look into what is causing the Honey on Earth to be affecting them Sir.' The voice stopped and took in an intake of breath.

What?! Thought The President. A planet called Delavia? Bigfoot is an alien? But some live on Earth. Something about bees AND *a portal on Earth!*

'I'm sorry,' said The President. 'Did you say a portal on our Earth?'

'Yes Sir'

'A portal on his world comes through to a portal on our world?' The President said in disbelief. It was hard to swallow. 'Where is it?'

'Apparently so Sir. The creature said that there are several of these things on our planet but that we have lost the knowledge of them over time and the ability to open them Sir. Apparently the one he comes through to access our planet is based in Oregon Sir.'

'Oregon?' Of all places. The President swallowed. His head was spinning. From a security perspective this was a nightmare. What did he do with that information? How did they defend the Earth if more of these creatures wanted to come through? Particularly if they didn't even know where these portals were? And what about other creatures from other worlds? Were there other worlds? Could they come through to Earth too? This was too much. The President felt sick. He had left this kind of stuff to the MJ17 Faction as this was their bag. However he thought, this has now been brought to my attention specifically, so as the President of the United States I cannot ignore this. I have to do something, even if I am stepping on someone else's toes. The fact that he didn't even know who this 'someone' was rankled with him a bit.

There were organisations and factions within the United States like MJ17 that did things in terms of looking after the security of the nation, that even he was not aware of. This disturbed him a bit. How could he govern a country, if he wasn't aware of everything that he was governing? Did the MJ17 Faction know about the existence of these portals? He wiped at his brow with a hanky. He just realised that he was sweating.

'I want you to find out how many of these portal things there are on the planet and where they are and I want you to get me this information as soon as possible.' The President tried to keep his voice calm when every fibre of his being was beginning to panic.

'Yes Sir,' said the monotone voice on the other end of the phone.

'I also want you to make sure that you go on this expedition and report back to me everything that happens.' The President said desperately.

'Yes Sir, ah Sir there is one more piece of information,' the voice hesitated.

Oh god what now, 'Yes what is it.' The President swallowed.

'They are taking a 15 year old American girl from Oregon with them Sir on the mission. An Isadora Stone Sir. She is apparently the Sasquatch's acquaintance.'

Figures! Laughed The President inside. I, the President of the United States only find out today that the Sasquatch is real and yet a 15 year old American girl is best friends with it. You need to get more down with the kids. Actually I do he thought. When was the last time you had a long chat with your own kids? And your Grandkids? Guilt washed over him in waves. Too busy running the country hey, he laughed inwardly. He made the decision that after this call he would go and track his Grandkids down and remind them that he could still have fun.

'OK, thanks for the update. Find out as much as you can for me on this Isadora Stone and why they think she will be useful to the mission and report everything back as soon as you have anything new.' The President tried to make his voice sound positive.

'OK Sir.' The line went dead.

I knew there would be some surprises when I took this job he thought. But Sasquatch who are friends with American girls who live on another world to Earth, was not one of them. Neither was Portals on Earth. The President frowned.

That could be a problem. A *big* problem.

6.00pm – Isadora's Home, Phelps Creek, Oregon

Isadora, Chinga and Mrs Stone were all tucking into their second bowl of Mrs Stones famous Mac and Cheese. The secret she said was putting bacon in it. Chinga was without question addicted to Honey. But he felt after eating two bowls of Mrs Stones Mac and Cheese that he quite possibly could have become addicted to that too.

'Could I trouble you for another bowl of this Mac and Cheese please Mrs Stone,' said Chinga politely.

'Yes of course!' Mrs Stone beamed and she jumped up to pile more gooey, unctuous cheesy pasta into Chinga's blue bowl.

Isadora was so happy. She couldn't remember when she had felt as happy as this for a long time. She didn't know what made her the most happy. Seeing her Momma back to normal again and excitedly, and busily buzzing around the kitchen, making yummy food. Or seeing a massive Sasquatch sat at her dining room table eating Mac and Cheese. She stifled a giggle. If you had told me yesterday that I would be sat at my kitchen table eating Mac and Cheese that Momma had made with Chinga, I wouldn't have believed it, she thought.

The reason they were sat at Isadora's kitchen table eating Mac and Cheese was that they had some time to kill before the portal opened again in order to travel to Chinga's world. And also Isadora had refused to go anywhere with anyone until she had seen with her own eyes that her Momma was indeed better. As she watched her Momma singing whilst she started washing the pots, she was satisfied that this was the case. Orion was fantastic she thought. How will I ever repay him?

Fortunately for Isadora. Mrs Stone had always been very open minded. And in view of this, it wasn't too traumatic to introduce a 9 foot Sasquatch to her. Mrs Stone had simply took it all in her stride and invited him in for tea. Isadora had told her Momma that Chinga was her friend and she had met him whilst star gazing in the woods. This it would seem was enough information to satisfy Mrs Stone who had always been in touch with her spiritual side.

As Isadora contemplated whether she had room for some of her Momma's incredible Chocolate Cream Pie, her mind wandered to the task that they were to face tomorrow. Tomorrow Chinga, Orion, Robin, Mike, Isadora and a bunch of other scientists and doctors would be waiting for a 'portal' to open that would somehow transport them all to Chinga's planet. Chinga knew where this portal could be found, and he would show them all tomorrow. Apparently it was in the woods at the back of her house near to where she had first met him. Presumably that day when she had first met Chinga, he had been on his way back to the portal to go home.

She was nervous. She had obviously never left her planet before. She laughed inside, who had? But now she had her Momma 'back' she was scared to leave her again. She had told her Momma that she was going on a school trip for Geography tomorrow and her Momma had swallowed this. That was the beauty of Mrs Stone, she never had asked questions. She just believed what her daughter told her implicitly. She didn't even ask why the huge Sasquatch would be going on the Geography trip too. I mean she'd only just met him right, but he was going on a Geography trip with school too? Isadora felt a twinge of guilt, she didn't like lying to her Momma. And part of her wondered why she didn't have a Momma who asked more questions. But this had to be done, and it was best that Mrs Stone did not ask questions. She had to help Chinga and his people and the only way to do that was to find out what was going on.

As she looked at both her Momma and Chinga. She wanted to savor this moment with them. To stop time. To bottle it so she could always remember how happy she was feeling. She swallowed a bubble of sadness. How strange that you could feel happy and sad all at the same time.

'Momma, I will have some Chocolate Cream Pie please' Isadora sighed. Mrs Stone beamed.

Delavia

The next morning, Isadora was looking through her clothes deciding what to pack in the small ruck sack that she was taking. She had no idea how long they would be gone or what the weather would be like on Chinga's planet. What should she pack? She couldn't fit much in her bag so she needed to pack something that she could definitely use. And she wasn't lugging a bigger bag.

'Chinga what is your planet like? What kind of clothes will I need to pack?' Isadora asked the huge furry creature as he was looking intently through her sneaker collection. Sasquatch didn't wear shoes and it would seem that he was fascinated by them.

'Delavia is beautiful,' said the big creature wistfully. 'Just beautiful. It is one of the most beautiful planets in the Cosmos. That's why we left Earth to go live there. It has lush golden vegetation and huge tall trees that go on for miles. Beautiful waterfalls and crystal clear lakes. If I could liken it to any place on your planet that is similar. It is a bit like the place that you call Canada. But much more beautiful and lush. And there are different colours on Delavia than there are on Earth. A lot of the plants are golden'.

Isadora could not imagine anything more beautiful than Canada. Although she had never been there. She had seen pictures on the internet of the iconic lakes shrouded by trees, and the bears fishing for salmon that were swimming upstream. She had always thought that it would be a place that she would love to visit at some point.

'Where does that amazing Candy come from that you always bring me? Asked Isadora. Will I be able to get some whilst we are there?' Isadora really hoped that they could. It was the most delicious thing that she had ever tasted.

'That Candy is considered to be a real delicacy on our planet. It is made from the Honey of the original bees that were taken from your planet years ago, which are looked after and owned by the Ancients on Delavia. The bees make the Honey from the flowers that grow on Delavia. That is what makes the Candy taste so wonderful. As Delavia has the most beautiful flowers in the Universe.' Explained the huge hairy creature whilst trying to get his foot in Isadora's sneaker without much success.

'We have a flower on our planet which is known as the Delavian Korona. It is a beautiful, huge, bright red flower which the bees love as it is so very sweet and it makes the most delicious Honey'.

'But if your Honey on Delavia is so good, why do you come to Earth to get ours?' asked Isadora.

It didn't make sense. Hang on, she remembered him mentioning something about the Ancients keeping it for themselves?

A frown spread over Chinga's face. 'The Ancients control all the bees on our planet and they are greedy. They eat almost all the Honey that the bees produce. They only leave enough for the bees to eat to keep them alive. And they allow enough to be taken to create the Candy that you have tasted, which they use on our planet to barter for things. Because of this there is not much of the Candy made, it is very rare. The Ancients use the Candy to barter for other things that they want. Like if they want someone to come and clip their nails, they will pay them in Candy.' Isadora was trying to imagine a Sasquatch having their nails clipped and she stifled a giggle.

'How do you come by the Candy that you always bring me then if it is so rare?' asked Isadora. 'Do you work for the Ancients too?' She laughed. 'Do you clip their nails?'

'No!' exclaimed Chinga looking affronted that she would suggest that he was a nail clipper. 'I play cards with someone who clips the High Ancients feet. He's not very good at cards,' smiled Chinga, 'He keeps me in Candy!' Chinga's smile faded. 'But the ones of us which do not have access to the Candy or the Honey on Delavia. We have to come to Earth to get our 'fix'. Thousands of years ago, just a few of us knew about the Honey of Earth and how to get here. Those of us whose bloodlines came from the first settlers on Delavia. Now most of the population on Delavia have to sustain their habit by coming to Earth and taking your Honey. The males always do the journey just in case they get caught. It does not taste anywhere near as good as the Honey we have on Delavia. But we have no choice but to eat it. I guess you guys could liken it to your coffee.'

Isadora thought, Chinga really likes talking about coffee. She had never cared for it herself.

Chinga continued, 'It's the difference between having proper roast ground coffee that you humans seem to cherish, versus having a cup of instant coffee. The instant coffee will do. It will give you your fix and take the edge off your craving, but it does not substitute for having the real thing.'

Isadora took his word for it, she had no desire anytime soon to start drinking coffee. How did he know all this stuff?

'So the Ancients eat most of the Honey made by your bees, and the rest of you eat bits of Candy that they make. And then come to our world to get the rest of your Honey fix?' Isadora mused. 'But what else do you guys eat? You can't just live off Candy and Honey?' Isadora gestured to him. 'You're huge!'

Chinga laughed, 'There are other things that we eat on our planet, like shoots and greens. Delavia has lots of juicy plants that live on it,' his smile faded. 'But what we really love is Honey'.

Isadora and Chinga's conversation was interrupted by a loud knock at the door.

They were here.

Isadora swallowed and looked at Chinga, 'I'd better go and say goodbye to Momma'.

Isadora ran downstairs and opened the door, looking around for her Momma on her way there. She was nowhere to be seen.

On the other side of her front door stood Robin and Mike the Scientists from Area 51, Orion the handsome tall Cowboy, and three other people which Isadora hadn't met before. Isadora said Hi to Robin, Mike and Orion and then turned to study the three new people. One was a woman with huge horn-rimmed glasses. She had every colour in the spectrum displayed in her outfit in various different bits and pieces. She had huge curly red hair and large teeth. She was wearing a purple cardigan, a yellow and orange striped top, a green flowing skirt, red beads, blue shoes and a brown ruck sack. 'Hi,' she smiled lunging forward with her hand to shake Isadora's and tripping over her own feet. 'My name is Dr Lilly Davis. I'm a doctor, specialising specifically in animals.' She spat covering Isadora in spittle from her overly large teeth.

'Hi, I'm Isadora Stone and I'm err.....I'm Chinga's friend.'

'You are more than that Isadora,' said Orion aloud for everyone to hear, in his booming velvet voice. 'You are the key to the success of this mission, without you, we can't talk to the Ancients remember. You are not only human, so representative of the planet that is inadvertently poisoning their people, but you are also capable of communicating telepathically too?' Orion winked.

'Yeah of course, and what Orion said too,' Isadora laughed nervously.

'Fascinating,' laughed Dr Lilly Davis. 'So how does it work then? You just 'think' what you want to say to them and they hear it? Without you having to even open your mouth? How fantastic!' She laughed and snorted at the same time.

'Ah yes, something like that,' said Isadora. She was starting to feel embarrassed. How did it work? She didn't really know? She had just always heard Chinga in her head and it seemed that it worked this way with Orion too.

Another man to the left of Isadora's vision spoke next. 'I'm Dr Fred Wallis, I am also an animal doctor.' This man was very softly spoken and dressed in classic hiking gear. I guess you could say he was dressed for the task at hand, unlike Dr Lilly Davis. Isadora liked this man instantly. Isadora smiled at Dr Wallis as she shook his hand and he smiled back. 'Nice to meet you' Isadora heard in her head in a new male voice that she recognised as being Dr Fred Wallis'. Stifling a gasp, Isadora looked at Fred more closely. So you are an alien too? Isadora thought, Wow, How many of you are there?

'There are many of us here on Earth,' Dr Wallis replied directly into Isadora's head. 'We look just like you humans, and mingle right in. You do not even know we are here.' Wow, thought Isadora, this is crazy. I can't believe I can hear you? The knowledge unnerved Isadora a lot.

She had always known she was different as a child, she could often hear voices that other people quite obviously couldn't hear. She once had a conversation in a supermarket in her head with a nice old lady who was in the queue behind her and her Momma. It was only after they left the supermarket and Isadora had asked Mrs Stone if they could go and visit the nice old lady sometime, that she realised that it was only herself that had spoken to the lady. Mrs Stone didn't even know there was a woman behind them at all. It got her into trouble quite a few times as a child, but most people just put it down to childlike attention seeking and her 'acting out'. As she had got older, she learnt to keep quiet about the things that she could hear, which other people obviously couldn't. Most kids her age already thought she was a freak as she loved nature and books, not makeup and boys. She didn't want to remind them of this on a daily basis by talking about 'hearing voices' too.

'I don't want to interrupt whatever is going on here between you two but we really need to get a move on.' The third person that Isadora had never met before barked quite forcefully.

As she turned to stare at this rude man, Isadora realised that to everyone else, it looked like Dr Wallis and herself were just stood staring and smiling at each other. Red colour streaked up Isadora's chest and neck. She needed to learn how to use this gift properly. Although until yesterday, she hadn't really realised that it was a gift at all. More like a curse.

This guy who had barked the order was quite obviously a member of the Military. He had green camouflage type clothes on, and a very stern face. From his demeanor, Isadora could tell that he was in charge. Or at least he thought that he was.

'It's good to see that all of you have dressed for the mission.' The Military man said with sarcasm dripping from every word. He looked them all up and down with derision.

'Nobody mentioned a dress code?' Said Dr Lilly Davis adjusting her top and beads and looking highly affronted.

'Common sense soldier when advancing into enemy territory,' barked the angry man. 'Time is of the essence. Where is the creature, we have to go?'

'Soldier!' Dr Lilly Davis snorted bemusedly to Isadora. 'He sounds like he thinks were off to war instead of a peace keeping mission!' and she laughed loudly again whilst slightly spitting on Isadora's face.

Isadora frowned at the Military man whilst she wiped away the spittle. She resented the way he had said 'creature'. She guessed he meant Chinga. Chinga was not a creature. He was her friend. She did not like this man. He made every fibre of her being want to run in the opposite direction. Who was he? Where was Chinga? He had probably gone to say goodbye to her Momma and negotiate for some more recipes to take back to Delavia.

Isadora swallowed a wave of anguish when she thought about her Momma. What if she got ill again whilst she was away?

'She will not get ill ever again Isadora, of that I promise you.' Orion's masculine voice boomed in Isadora's head.

Her eyes flicked to Orion. He winked at her. She blushed.

Robin and Mike said in unison, 'How is Chinga?' Then they looked at each other and both giggled at the same time. They were both obviously desperate to see him again.

'I'll go and find him,' Isadora said aloud for the benefit of everyone. She bent her head low as she walked away, so Orion could not see the red colour gliding up her neck. Orion made her feel nervous, always.

She found Chinga in the living room with her Momma, trying to persuade Mrs Stone to divulge what the ingredients were for her Mac and Cheese.

'No Chinga,' laughed Mrs Stone. 'It's a family secret which I'm afraid I can't tell you'. Her eyes danced. She absolutely loved it when someone was trying to extract her cooking secrets from her.

'Ah Momma, I have to go now,' Isadora said to her Momma, as she knelt down to hug her.

'Oh OK,' said Mrs Stone her eyes filling with tears. 'I thought I heard voices, Are those your teachers?'

Teachers? Thought Isadora, what does she mean? Then she remembered that she was supposed to be going on a Geography trip.

'Ah yes Momma, they're my teachers,' Isadora lied guiltily. She kissed her Momma, hoping that everything was going to go well and that she would in fact get to see her again. It was not every day that you went through a magic portal into a different world. What happened if something went wrong and she somehow got split in half or something? She didn't know how these things worked! She told herself to stop being dramatic.

'Will you call me when you get there?' Mrs Stone asked.

Isadora looked at Chinga for help with this one. Would there be phones?

'Ah, she probably won't be able to call you Mrs Stone I'm afraid, the vegetation is too thick where we are going.' Chinga quickly lied.

'But we'll drop you an email as soon as we find somewhere with internet access.'

They have internet access? Isadora laughed internally. Of course, everyone does these days.

'I understand.' Said Mrs Stone. 'Well be careful and I can't wait to see you when you get back.'

'OK Momma, I love you.' Isadora kissed her Momma on the cheek and pulled her into a hug. She loved the smell of her Momma, She smelt like home. Always.

'I love you too Izzy,' Mrs Stone sniffed. She smothered kisses all over her daughters face, Like she used to when Isadora was a child.

'You've not called me Izzy since I was a little girl Momma,' Izzy smiled.

'You'll always be my little Izzy, no matter how big you get,' Mrs Stone teased and kissed her daughter again.

'Now off you go,' sniffed Mrs Stone. 'Your teachers are waiting.'

'OK Momma see you in a few days.' Isadora gave her Momma one last lingering glance and then turned to leave. She hated leaving her.

Isadora picked up her rucksack and started to put it on her shoulders whilst walking through the front door. Instantly, she could feel anger coming off the Military man in waves.

'Have you finished the pitiful goodbyes?' He barked. 'Can we go now before we miss this thing opening and then the whole mission will have to be aborted?' He turned on his heels as he spoke and stalked off into the woods at the back of Isadora's house. 'Follow me soldiers!' He shouted as he disappeared through the trees.

'Jeez,' said Isadora in disgust. 'Who IS that guy?'

Dr Lilly Davis shivered and let out a huge breath. 'He says his name is General Myers. I don't know who or what he is, but I wouldn't want to get on the wrong side of him.'

'No' Isadora thought as she set off at a sprint following after the General, 'me neither.'

The Portal

Chinga had caught up to General Myers along the way with his huge long legs and was now slightly in front of the General.

They were deep in the woods at the back of Isadora's home. Isadora loved the woods and had spent hours and hours in here as a child with her Daddy, looking for various different creatures and star gazing at night. But even she had never been quite this far into these woods. The vegetation was starting to get very dense.

Suddenly Chinga started to smell the air. General Myers held up his hand indicating for them all to stop in their tracks.

Chinga stepped forward into a place where the vegetation had been trampled down quite considerably. 'It is here,' Chinga whispered.

Ok, thought Isadora, there's nothing there? What happens now?'

Orion, Fred and Chinga all heard Isadora's thoughts, Orion was the first to answer. He answered aloud for the benefit of all.

'We wait for the bubble to appear, and then we step into it one at a time,' he explained. 'You will feel funny like your whole body is full of energy. When you come out the other side on Delavia, it is not unusual to feel sick.' Orion winked at Isadora as he said this.

Isadora immediately thought that there was no way that she wanted to be sick in front of Orion. Orion smiled.

Well that sounds simple Isadora thought? Sarcastically. What in the hell did that mean?

Chinga said 'I will go first just watch what I do. Walk into the bubble after me.'

OK, thought Isadora, so where is the bubble?

General Myers got out a stop watch. 'The portal will be open for 3 hours today, the General barked. If the mission takes longer then we have to wait till 1900 hours tomorrow night before the portal will open again. Therefore we will require an overnight stop in Delavia. Can you confirm that this will be OK creature?' The General shouted whilst looking disdainfully at Chinga.

'His name is Chinga!' Robin, Mike and Isadora all shouted at the same time.

The Generals face never changed. He still expected an answer.

'Yes that's fine,' Chinga smiled, speaking directly to Isadora and ignoring the General. 'I can introduce you to my family and you can stay the night at my hut.'

Isadora realised all at once that Chinga had never spoken to her about his family before. She had spoken at length to him about her Daddy disappearing and her Momma's subsequent decline. She'd even spoken to him about being bullied at school by Verity Ashworth and her gang. But when she had asked Chinga about his family, he had never gone into any details. She didn't even know how old he was? Suddenly she felt like she didn't know Chinga at all. Isadora started to feel really nervous.

The General started counting, 'OK soldiers, the portal will open in 5,4,3,2,1.'

No time to back out now Isadora thought.

Suddenly a bright shiny bubble appeared in the clearing above the trodden down grass. It was shimmering like the heat radiating off a highway in the height of summer.

Chinga set off walking forwards towards the bubble. As he stepped into the bubble, there was a sucking sound like something on the other side had sucked him through. All at once he disappeared into thin air. Isadora gawped in amazement.

'Miss Stone, you next please barked the General. Hurry, hurry.'

Isadora took a deep breath and started walking towards the bubble. What was she doing? As she got nearer to the centre of the bubble, her skin started to prickle and she felt a curious feeling entering her body. It was like the feeling you get after you've eaten a lot of Candy, and the sugar hits your brain. All of her muscles felt full of energy and she had a warm feeling in the pit of her stomach.

Suddenly, WHOOSH, Isadora was pulled through to Delavia with such a force she thought her head would spin off her shoulders. She instinctively shut her eyes and put her hands up to her face. It felt like there were thousands of threads attached to her that all pulled her forward at once. The ground left her feet and then all of a sudden the ground was there again. The first thing she was aware of was the sound of birds, but unlike any bird call she had ever heard before. It was more like music. She gingerly opened her eyes. Chinga was stood in front of her grinning and laughing his head off with his huge distinctive belly laugh.

'It feels a bit funny the first time you 'hop' doesn't it?' Chinga teased.

Isadora bent double and vomited all over the floor. As she did so she noticed that the floor was covered in the most beautiful flowers she had ever seen. The colours she could not describe. Some of these colours she had never ever seen on Earth before. And then it hit her, she wasn't on Earth any more. She was on Delavia.

Pop! The next person through the portal was Orion.

Perfect! Thought Isadora as she wiped the sick off her chin, and stood up straight.

'Don't worry Isadora, it affects us all like that the first time,' Orion teased and ruffled her hair. 'Although I can't remember my first time.' He said wiggling his eyebrows.

Isadora stepped back from Orion as she was worried she might throw up again. And she stank of vomit. Her face felt hot.

Pop! Next came Dr Lilly Davis who proceeded to vomit straight away just as Isadora had. At least she didn't feel as bad now, she thought. Then Robin, who also threw up. Mike shot through next and was looking really smug until he threw up so loud and hard that everyone went over to check he was OK. Finally Dr Wallis popped through followed by General Myers, both of whom did not seem to be effected by the 'hop' at all.

'Right *Chinga*,' General Myers sneered, 'lead the way please.'

Chinga set off walking at such a fast pace, that Isadora and the rest of the party struggled to keep up. He is obviously excited to show us where he lives Isadora thought, as she ran after him.

As she rushed through her surroundings she wanted to ask Chinga to slow down as Delavia was simply beautiful. It was almost golden. Shimmering golden, but all around them was vegetation and trees and flowers. The word that Chinga had used to describe it was correct. It was paradise. The floor was almost a carpet of flowers. Some of the most beautiful flowers that Isadora had ever seen or could ever imagine. She thought that Chinga was very generous in comparing Delavia to Canada.

All of a sudden she noticed that Chinga was quite far in front of them. Was she dawdling or had he picked up speed? She realised he was running. Why was he running she thought? Was something wrong?

The next sound she heard was Chinga screaming, 'NOOOOOOOOOO, NOOOOOOO, NOOOOOOO.' He was running, definitely running Isadora thought. What was going on?

Isadora set off running after Chinga, but was struggling to keep up with the huge Sasquatch. His legs were considerably longer than Isadora's, but she managed to keep him in her eye sight until he disappeared into some trees. Isadora shot after Chinga and burst out through the trees and into a huge clearing in a wooded area on the other side.

All at once she realised why Chinga was so upset. She had been so disorientated when coming through the portal and into Chinga's world, and her senses had been so bombarded with all the new sights and sounds, that she hadn't realised that there was a familiar smell in the air. The smell was the smell of burning. She felt and understood Chinga's panic. Her eyes couldn't quite take in the horror of the scene. It seemed that everywhere was on fire.

Isadora took in the scene, her mouth open wide. There were thousands of wooden huts built on stilts in this clearing. Thousands of them. This must be Chinga's village, Isadora thought. All of these huts were on fire or were smouldering from having been on fire.

In the centre of the clearing, in the middle of all the smouldering huts, sat around a camp fire and laughing and joking, were about 100 *huge*, really ugly creatures. They had green skin and were dressed all in brown. Their clothing looked to be a leather type of material, with silver bullets and weapons strapped all round their bodies. They had the ugliest faces Isadora had ever seen with huge noses and lips and long, droopy ears. Their heads were basically bald with little wisps of white hair, sporadically sticking up off their grotesque heads. Their teeth were huge, yellow and disgusting. But the thing that struck Isadora the most about these creatures, was that they were massive. Absolutely massive. They were all of them the size of a house at least. Then something else caught her eye. Up in the sky to the side of the clearing where they were stood, was the biggest spaceship she had ever seen in her life. Not that she had ever seen a spaceship before in real life, she thought. It looked like the ship on Independence Day. It was gigantic. All in a pitch black colour with huge spikes sticking out of it across the front, the back and all along the top ridge. It was the scariest thing that Isadora had ever seen. Her chest constricted with anxiety. What was happening? She looked at Chinga who had tears streaming down his furry, brown face and was sobbing enormous heavy wracking sobs.

'Why?' Chinga screamed.

'Chinga!' Isadora cried. 'What has happened here? What are those huge things? Have you seen that ship? What is happening?' Isadora thought she may start crying. This was all a bit too much to take in. Two days ago she had been just a normal (ish) school girl studying

Maths, being scolded for not listening in class. And now she was stood on a different planet to Earth, staring at huge grotesque giants. In front of a massive scary spaceship, having just come through a portal. She thought she might be sick again.

'No time for explanations Miss Stone our cover has been blown. We need to leave now!' shouted General Myers. He pointed to the group of ugly creatures who had turned towards Chinga's screams and were now getting up and slowly starting to lumber in their direction. Isadora noticed that all of these hideous things were carrying giant black weapons of some kind, which were shimmering. They were unfamiliar to her.

'Run,' screamed the General. 'Back to the portal quick!'

They all set off running back to the portal, Isadora grabbed Chinga's hand and pulled him into a run as he was stood rooted to the spot with a mask of horror on his face. Screaming.

'My Family!' Chinga screamed. 'I need to find them!'

'There aren't enough of us Chinga, we need to go back to Earth and bring reinforcements.' Isadora shouted over the noise of the fires and screaming. She noticed that there was a huge pen containing what looked to be a lot of Chinga's kind.

Chinga would not move. 'Chinga, we will come back, I promise!' Screamed Isadora. 'You can't help them now, we will be killed, but if we go back and get reinforcements then we stand a chance at being able to save them!'

Chinga looked at Isadora and something changed in his eyes. 'OK, run!' he screamed.

Chinga and Isadora set off running towards the portal, bursting through the trees. They could see Orion stood by the shimmering bubble. 'Quick, hurry!' Orion shouted. 'I can close the portal so they can't follow us to Earth, but you need to hurry.'

From behind them the sounds of these creatures got louder. Isadora could hear the thunderous clatter of their feet as they started to run. She ran harder than she had ever run in her life. She felt like her lungs would pop out of her chest.

Dr Lilly Davis, Dr Fred Wallis and General Myers had all jumped through the portal but Orion was waiting for them in front of the shimmering bubble. Isadora reached the bubble first and jumped straight into it. Again the threads pulled her through so hard and so violently that she felt like she would die. As quick as she had jumped into the bubble, she was spat out again. Back in the woods at the back of her own house. Time seemed to slow down and speed up all at once.

She picked herself up and got out of the way. Next pop, Chinga was sucked through the bubble and he sat down on the floor with his head in his hands. Isadora immediately ran and sat down next to him and tried to comfort him. But her thoughts were on Orion. Where was he? He said he was going to stay and close the portal? How could he do that? Was he OK? This was taking a long time. Her heart started to pound harder in her chest. Something was wrong. This was taking too long.

Suddenly, pop, Orion was sucked through the bubble and the bubble folded in on itself and disappeared. He looked effortlessly gorgeous as usual and smiled as he saw Isadora's anguished face and read her thoughts. 'Don't worry Isadora,' smiled Orion with his dazzling smile. 'I always land on my feet.' He ruffled her hair again but with a more serious look on his face than normal.

'What did you do to the portal?' Isadora asked Orion trying the change the subject.

'There is a way that you can close it behind you, if you know how. I have been round long enough to know how. It won't open again till later and when it does it won't go to Earth for a long time,' Orion whispered in Isadora's ear. God he smelt good. Orion laughed.

Isadora's thoughts were interrupted with a scream of anger that emanated from her Sasquatch friend

'Chinga,' Isadora said softly. 'What has just happened here? What *were* those things? They were gigantic?'

'He must have come because we're vulnerable at the moment,' Chinga sobbed. 'We're not able to defend ourselves like normal because we are all getting sick. But how did he know?' He resumed crying huge heavy sobs.

'Who,' barked General Myers. 'Who are you talking about soldier?'

Chinga's sobs had died down and he was now just whimpering. He wiped a huge trail of snot off the end of his nose and down along the brown fur on his arm.

'Valdazar!' Chinga cried, and uncontrollable sobs broke out of Chinga's chest with renewed vigour.

Area 51, Nevada

General Myers had organised their transport back to the Hanger room at Area 51 with incredible efficiency.

Isadora could not believe that they were back where this had all started two days ago, and they had not achieved anything at all.

They were all sat round the table and General Myers was leading the conversation. He was *not* happy that their mission had been a resounding failure. Not happy at *all*.

'What has just happened here soldier?' General Myers shouted at Chinga.

'Valdazar,' sniffed Chinga softly. 'He has taken Delavia.'

'Yes you've already said that,' barked the General. 'But who or what is Valdazar?'

Chinga leant forward and took a sip of water from a plastic cup which was on the table. It looked like a little thimble in the giant creatures hands. He almost could not hold onto it as his hands were shaking so violently.

'Valdazar has taken Delavia as he has somehow found out that we have all been getting sick. He knows we are weak and that we couldn't defend ourselves. He has taken our moment of weakness and maximised on it. He has taken Delavia for himself. And what a prize Delavia is.' Fresh tears leaked out of Chinga's eyes.

'Who is Valdazar Chinga?' Robin asked softly. She wiped the huge Sasquatch's tears away that were dripping down the fur on his face.

Chinga took in a deep breath and looked at Robin. 'Valdazar is pure evil. He is the leader of the Valdons. They are from the planet Valdar. Valdar is a huge gas planet in a Solar system, in a Galaxy next to our Galaxy.'

'He's not from our Galaxy?' Mike asked quizzically. What the hell did that mean? Mike thought.

'No,' said Chinga in an angry voice. 'What most of you humans don't seem to realise yet, and I don't understand why the rest of your kind have not explained this to you? As some of you know for sure! It's so strange to me! Our Universe is teeming with life. Absolutely teeming. All of the planets, in all of the Solar systems, in all of the galaxies have life on or in them. You humans are one of the *last* 'beings' that have evolved in the Universe. Yet you think you own it all and there is only you here! It makes me so angry.' Chinga spat.

Isadora had never seen Chinga like this before. Why was he so angry, particularly with humans? They gave him the Honey right? What was going on here? Although the Honey had made them sick, maybe that was why he was so mad.

'So Valdazar lives on a planet that is not in our Solar system or even our Galaxy?' Said Robin. 'Wow that's incredible.'

'Yes it's *wonderful*,' shouted Chinga sarcastically. 'And now he's taken over my home.'

'Why would he have done that Chinga?' asked Isadora. 'What does he want? Is Valdar not enough for him?'

Chinga sighed. 'Valdazar has slowly taken over every planet within his Solar system, one by one. Then after that he started taking over other planets in other Solar systems, neighbouring his. Now it looks like he has moved into our Galaxy too, and Delavia is definitely the 'prize' of our Galaxy. Delavia is paradise.'

Nobody in the room could argue with that.

'Why does Valdazar keep taking over all these planets?' Questioned Robin? 'What is it that he wants?'

Chinga looked down at his huge hands. 'Valdazar takes whatever he can to trade. It's all about trade and power. The Valdons are a stupid, war mongering race and they just do whatever he says. He takes things from civilisations and trades them with other civilisations, for the newest and most innovative Technology. He always wants to have the best weapons and the best ships and the best of everything. But he doesn't make any of it himself, he just takes it. He is evil and a bully. And now he has my family. My children!' Chinga started sobbing again but this time it was a heart broken wail. Isadora's heart broke for her friend. What could she do to help?

'What can we do to defeat this Valdazar and save your family Chinga?' Asked Isadora. Her heart broke when she thought about Chinga's children being kept in that huge pen that they had seen. What would be his weakness? What were those creatures? They were enormous. 'Is Valdazar even bigger than the rest of them if he is their leader?' Isadora asked. Trying to imagine how big he would have to be, she shivered.

Chinga looked at Isadora. He looked at her like he was seeing her for the first time. He laughed. A strange laugh. He laughed so hard that he almost fell backwards off his chair. A huge big belly laugh which ricocheted around the room like gun fire. His laughter sounded so very strange.

'You have no idea have you?' wailed Chinga, as his laughter turned once again into tears.

'Valdazar isn't a Valdon!' He screamed.

'Valdazar is not even *from* Valdar.'

Chinga laughed again incredulously, 'Valdazar is *Human*!'

The Revelation

Everyone around the table sat and looked at Chinga incredulously. Valdazar, the evil being who was taking over the planets one by one, and had now moved into our Galaxy..........was human?

 How could that be?

 'Valdazar is human?' Barked General Myers. 'Is this a joke soldier?'

 'No,' laughed Chinga, wiping his eyes. 'I wish it was. Valdazar is Human. No-one knows how he ended up on Valdar. It is assumed that he 'hopped' there. Some of your kind do know about these portals you know?' The big Sasquatch exclaimed, looking round the room in surprise. 'The Valdons are a big stupid race. They are easily led and they are obsessed with Technology. So if Valdazar has somehow hopped to their planet and then promised them new Technology through war mongering, then they will listen to him. They don't have the intelligence to figure these things out on their own. But Valdazar is pure evil. With his brains and intent and the Valdons strength and willingness to blindly follow everything that Valdazar says, together they make a lethal and winning combination.'

 'So what do we do now?' Isadora said, looking round the room.

 'I have to go back,' Chinga said sadly. 'I have to free my people and see if I can find my family. My mate Lamay. My two children Peets and Sneets. I hope it is not too late.' His eyes swam with tears again.

 Isadora felt sick thinking about Chinga's children trapped in that pen and the village slowly smouldering away. They had to save them.

 'We need reinforcements, and we need a new plan of attack in place soldier,' barked the General.

 'Wait,' said Mike, 'you said that these Valdons are obsessed with Technology right?'

'Yes' Chinga sniffed. 'They have the most up to date weapons that they can barter for in the Universe right now'.

'So if we're going to go back and defeat him and take Delavia back, should we not also have weapons that are at least as good so we have a level playing field?' Mike mused. 'I feel like we're getting out of our depth a bit here, what do you think Robin?' Mike asked his research partner. 'We're scientists not soldiers? I don't think we should be getting involved in this at all,' Mike continued. 'This has turned into something else entirely now.'

Robin agreed with Mike, this did seem like it was way above their pay grade. She wasn't up for being involved in any war. She was a Scientist. Hell she didn't even own a gun!

Robin cleared her throat, 'Ah hmmm. I think there needs to be a new strategy put in place for what we do now to help Chinga. Chinga obviously needs help in taking back his home. I feel that that is something that is maybe the General's area of expertise, not ours?'

All eyes went to the angry General, who was for the first time looking like he was the cat that got the cream.

'Yes, this is my area of expertise. I will arrange the ground troops, but we need to find a way to get there. We're not going to have much of an element of surprise, if we all have to file one by one through that portal of yours!' The General sniggered.

Orion had been sat back on his chair throughout this entire conversation with his Cowboy hat over his face. Isadora had thought at one point that he had gone to sleep. Suddenly he sat forward and tipped his Cowboy hat back up. The entire table had his attention. He was breathtakingly handsome. 'What y'all need is help. And flying Technology,' he drawled. 'And it just so happens that I have some, let's call them 'acquaintances', that might have the tools to do the job.' He smiled.

'We need to go ask them if they will help,' Orion explained. 'We need to go now if we are going to stand a chance of helping our hairy friend here. So who's coming?' Orion asked sensing that some people around the table were no longer up for the mission.

Chinga straight away said 'Count me in of course.' Isadora also said 'yes'. There was no way she was leaving her friend in the lurch now, not when he needed her help. Robin and Mike looked at each other and mutually decided that they would be best placed staying here at the lab and looking into what was going on with the Honey. They exchanged knowing glances. Isadora couldn't blame them. She didn't particularly want to get shot at either, but she was going to help her friend.

In the confusion of everything, pretty much everyone had forgotten about the real reason of why they had gone to Delavia in the first place. The Honey situation.

Dr Lily Davis and Dr Fred Wallis also agreed that they would probably be best placed staying with Robin and Mike and working on the Honey situation. So that just left General Myers.

'Of course I will be coming with you soldier, you need back up. I will sort out the reinforcements that we need for our mission on route to our new destination,' the General paused.

'Where is our destination soldier?' The General barked at Orion. Orion tipped his hat back up,
 'We need to go and see my friends, The Greys'.
Isadora gulped.

Delavia

Valdazar tipped his head back and laughed. A loud, evil, nasty laugh. Ha! He thought, that was too easy! Actually he hated it when it was easy. He preferred it when they put up a bit of fight. It made the victory all the more satisfying.

These pathetic creatures had basically rolled over straight away and given their planet up. This victory was particularly sweet! Ha! Sweet he thought! Literally! As now I control all the Delavian Honey. A delicacy renowned throughout the Universe. He laughed and leaned back on his throne. This throne came with him everywhere. Everywhere he conquered. He sat on this throne. It was made of Serantium. The most precious material in the Universe. It was precious as it was the perfect material for making spaceships out of. It molded into whatever shape you wanted it to, whenever you wanted it to. You only had to *think* it. He decided to change his throne into a dragon. The second he had the thought, the silver throne that he was sat on started shimmering and looked like it was changing into liquid. The throne then slowly changed into a huge silver dragon, all whilst Valdazar was still sat on it. From behind the head of the dragon, Valdazar surveyed his prize. The huge stupid 'Ancients', were locked in a mammoth makeshift pen that they'd had to create to contain them. Luckily Delavia was full of trees so he'd had some of the Valdons chop some down and make this thing as soon as they'd 'taken' the planet. It was fortunate that the Valdons were gigantic so the task had not been a difficult one.

Valdazar stared at the 'Ancients'. Man they were ugly. They were colossal, flabby beasts. Over time with eating large quantities of Delavian Honey, these things had grown so large, you could barely decipher where any of their body parts were. They were just a humongous flabby mess of brown hair with a head plonked on top.

Valdazar laughed. They looked so shocked and worried. I bet they wished they hadn't eaten so much of that Honey now! They had no visible legs left to run off with! How much of this Honey had they been eating? I mean to get that fat, you've got to be eating a *lot* of Honey right?

'Human!' Valdazar shouted for his telepath.

'Yes Sire,' Human said softly as he came out of the shadows from behind Valdazar's dragon. He kneeled in front of his Master.

'Ask those *fat blobs* where the Honey is. I want to try some of this *Delavian Honey* and see what is so special about it,' Valdazar spat.

'Yes Sire', Human turned round to face the Ancients. To anyone else in the room it just looked like Human and these huge fat creatures were staring at each other, but they were in fact having a full blown conversation, albeit telepathically.

Human turned to speak to his master. 'The Ancient ones have said that the bees are kept in a huge wooden hive at the back of their wooden palace. They are trapped in at night by a powerful force field that goes up around the hive. They are let out again first thing in the morning to go and procure nectar. The reason they are trapped in at night is in order to stop anyone trying to steal......'

'Yes, yes, yes, Human,' spat Valdazar. 'I didn't ask for a history of their civilisation. I asked where the Honey was.'

'Yes Master,' Human said sadly looking at the floor and he once again merged back into the shadows.

'You two!' Valdazar shouted at the two nearest Valdons who were guarding him. They snapped to attention out of a bored revere. They were for some reason, absolutely petrified of Valdazar, even though they were at least 20 times his size.

'Go and fetch me some of this special, *Delavian Honey*,' he sneered.

'Let's see why my *merchant friends* are willing to give me whatever I want for it'. He leant back on his shimmering dragon, and laughed menacingly.

The Underground

Isadora was currently sat open mouthed on an underground Tram system which apparently ran underneath the entire of the United States. Isadora was astounded that this thing even existed. I mean, if people knew that they could get from Nevada to Washington in 30 minutes flat, what would they think?

Orion was sat watching Isadora intently. He smiled, 'It's impressive isn't it?! It's been built for quite a while now. It was hell trying to get anywhere before. He leaned forwards and winked at her Especially in rush hour!' He whispered.

Isadora sat back in her seat putting some space between them. 'I just can't believe this thing exists? And how fast it is!'

'Yes' said Orion. 'We'll be there in 3 minutes.'

So the whole journey has taken about 8 minutes Isadora thought. From taking the lift at Area 51 into the lowest level that was off limits to practically everyone. And then getting on this thing which prior to 10 minutes ago, she had no idea existed.

The mind boggles she thought. What else was being hidden below ground from the American people?

'Ah a LOT of underground bases!' Orion laughed.

'I'm sorry?' Isadora said.

'You asked what *else* was being hidden below ground from the American people, and I said a LOT of underground bases,' Orion drawled.

Isadora needed to get used to Orion permanently invading her thoughts.

'What are the underground bases for?' Isadora asked curiously.

'Some are so they can carry out their operations covertly, without the prying eyes of the American people' Orion explained. Others, they're stock piling things. Food, weapons, animals, you name it, they've got it down there.'

'Why?' Isadora asked puzzled. 'Why do we need to stockpile food and animals? And weapons?' Isadora felt sick.

'I'll leave that one for you to work out Isadora,' Orion said quietly. 'They are your people.'

Their conversation was interrupted by the abrupt stopping of the underground Tram.

Isadora had been so overwhelmed by the Tram itself and engrossed in her conversation with Orion, that she realised that she had no idea where they were actually going.

'Where are we Orion?' Isadora asked reticently.

'We are in Dulce, New Mexico Isadora,' Orion drawled.

'At the Earth Base of what you humans love to call *The Greys.*'

Earth Base? Thought Isadora.

They have a base on Earth? What the hell?

Delavian Honey

Valdazar sat licking Honey off of his long, bony fingers.

'Unbelievable,' he cried. ' I can see why everyone wants this stuff, it's amazing! It's like, it's like nothing I've ever tasted! It's so sweet.' He guzzled down another mouthful. 'And this stuff is going to get me my new spaceship,' the deranged leader spat and laughed at the same time. 'The merchants are *desperate* for this stuff,' he chuckled. 'They will give me *whatever* I ask for! And I want that ship!' Valdazar whispered. He pictured the spaceship that the merchants had turned up in at their last trade meeting with him. It was unlike nothing that Valdazar had ever seen before. It was magnificent and he *wanted* it.

The Ancients looked longingly at the Honey dripping off the deranged conquerors fingers.

'So what have we done with the rest of the furry things then?' Valdazar sneered, gesturing to the Ancients. 'The small ones of course.'

'We've made some smaller pens Sire, similar to this.' One of the huge, grotesque Valdons said. 'The smaller ones are being held in there. Ah Sire, it appears that a lot of them are, urh..sick.'

'Sick?' Exclaimed Valdazar. 'What do you mean sick?' he said slurping more Honey from the huge pot that he had.

'They say it's something to do with the Honey Sire,' the huge Valdon said quietly.

Valdazar spat out the contents of his mouth. 'You idiot! He screamed, didn't you think to tell me that *before* I ate half of the pot!' Valdazar threw the pot and the remaining contents at the Valdon who had dared to give him the bad news. He jumped out of the way just in time before it connected with him.

'Ah no Sire,' said the second Valdon. 'It's not the Delavian Honey. It's the Honey from a place called Earth.'

'What did you say?' said Valdazar in shock, his voice lowering in disbelief.

'Ah – it's the Honey from Earth Sire. Not from Delavia, that is making them all sick.'

Valdazar stood there with his mouth open staring at the huge, talking idiot.

The Valdons looked at each other and then back at Valdazar. What was their master staring at?

Earth. It had been so long since he had heard that word mentioned.

'*Earth*' Valdazar said the word aloud. He felt the word leave his tongue and hang in the air.

Earth, yes of course, Valdazar thought. It had been so long, and he was a young boy when it all happened. But, yes, he remembered Earth. He remembered it well now he thought about it. But he hadn't thought about Earth in a long time. He had tried to block it from his memory. Put as many battles and conquests as possible between himself and Earth. Earth was when he had been a boy. And now he was the great Valdazar. The ruler of the Valdons. The conqueror of multiple planets and Solar systems. He was invincible. And he was the leader of a huge army of brutal giants who would do anything that he asked.

'Fetch me more Honey', he yelled. He sat back on his throne and began hatching a new plan.

Update

It had been too long since The President had heard from the JSOC operative, what was going on?

Had the mission been a success? Or were they still there?

The anticipation and suspense was killing him.

Suddenly the strange phone rang. The President jumped up to get it.

'Yes this is The President,' he said hurriedly.

The monotone voice of the Joint Special Operations Command operative started to speak.

'There's been a problem Mr President.'

'Problem, what problem', said The President.

'I'm not entirely sure Sir as we were unable to send anyone with them due to the quickness with which they arranged their mission. But almost immediately after them returning back through the portal, they have accessed the underground Tram system to Dulce, New Mexico Sir,' the operative droned.

'Dulce, New Mexico,' said The President quizzically. 'Why on Earth would they be going there? He wracked his brains. What did we have at Dulce New Mexico?' he thought.

'We believe they are attempting to access 'The Greys' headquarters on Earth Sir,' the voice enlightened.

What? thought The President. The Greys as in 'aliens'. The Grey's base on Earth? These things live in the sky right?

'I'm sorry, you said 'The Greys' base on Earth,' The President repeated to his Joint Special Operations Command operative. 'I must have heard you wrong, you mean their spaceship?'

'No Sir,' said the operative, 'The Greys' have a station on Earth, based in Dulce, New Mexico. It's underground Sir.'

The President stared into space.

Aliens have a base in Dulce New Mexico. In America. The America that he pledged to defend and protect. And he was just finding out about it.

What else didn't he know?

And he was the President of the United States.

'I will give you an update when I have any more information Sir,' said the operative making it clear that their conversation was over.

'Yes, yes please do.'

He sat and stared into space, numb. What do I do now?

The Greys

Isadora, Chinga, Orion and General Myers all disembarked from the underground Tram system. What did they do now? Isadora thought and shuddered as the Tram sped off down the track and into the distance at record speed. She couldn't believe she had just been on that thing.

Orion turned to face his three companions.

'OK folks listen up y'all. I have dealt with the Greys for many years. They are 'acquaintances' of mine you could say. So I would appreciate it if you just keep quiet and let me deal with the negotiations.' Orion directed his glare at General Myers.

The General frowned, obviously understanding the meaning behind Orion's words. Orion meant him. The General said nothing and checked his weapons.

Orion continued, 'The Greys have been here on this planet longer than you humans. There are various different types of beings that have been lumped under the term 'The Greys'. But the ones we have come to see today are the Reticulans who come from the Star System Zeta Reticuli. There are several types of 'Grey's that come from Zeta, these are just one branch of em I guess you could say. These ones see themselves as far more intelligent and worthy than humans. So don't give them any more reason to carry on believing this,' Orion said, again looking at the General.

This time the General took the bait. 'Have you got something to say soldier? If so just come out and say it so we can get in there, and get this over with. And win this war,' he barked.

'That is exactly my point General Myers,' Orion laughed. 'These Reticulans are a race of beings who have been here on the planet a lot longer than you surface humans. They consider this planet to be theirs. If you go in all guns blazing, this could start a war right here and now!' Orion raised his voice slightly. 'We do not want that do we General, as we are here to ask the Greys for their help. Remember! That is why we are here. We are here to ask the Greys for their help so we can use their ships to go and take Delavia back from Valdazar. *Not* start a war on Earth. Am I making myself clear?' Orion said quite loud. Isadora had never heard Orion use a stern voice before. Isadora thought it made him look even more handsome.

The General frowned again and opened his mouth like he was about to shout back, and then thought better of it. He closed his mouth and took in a deep breath. 'Understood loud and clear soldier. The directive is to secure the Technology so we can go and blast Valdazar off of Delavia. You can count on me not to start a war here and now soldier.'

Orion let out a huge breath. 'OK, so everyone just keep quiet and I will handle negotiations with Ebanon.'

'Who is Ebanon?' asked Isadora noticing that one of her laces was undone. She bent down to fasten her shoe.

'Ebanon is the Head Grey of this faction,' said Orion leaning down to take Isadora's hand and help her up. He held onto her hand. 'He controls them all. The large ones are all individuals but they have to do what he says. The smaller ones are Clones and do everything that he says without thinking for themselves. They are incapable of doing anything independently unless Ebanon sanctions it.'

Orion let go of Isadora's hand, just as she was starting to feel uncomfortable.

'OK,' said Isadora. 'Let's go meet Ebanon.'

They turned to face the hole of a tunnel that led off into the darkness.

Ebanon

Orion led the way down the pitch black corridor, which had branched off from the underground Tram station. Orion had pressed a button on his belt and it had promptly lit up with three very small, very powerful lights. It was these lights that illuminated their way as they walked down the pitch black corridor. This had been much to the amusement of General Myers, who clearly already thought that Orion was a bit of a joke.

'You'd think they'd have some sort of light on, so we could see where we were going.' Moaned Chinga as he tripped over his own huge, furry foot.

'That's the whole point my furry friend,' laughed Orion. 'They do not want *visitors* at all. And if they do have visitors, they don't want them to be able to see where they are going, until Ebanon has decided whether they are allowed to be let in or not.'

'You mean Ebanon can see us now?' Isadora said wondering how that would be given that the tunnel was pitch black.

'You mean to say this alien creature doesn't even know we are coming soldier?' Hissed the General. 'What if we are attacked?'

'If Ebanon was going to attack us General, trust me we would be dead already,' Orion shot back. 'In any case, Ebanon will have recognised my belt,' he smirked.

Presently they arrived at the end of the corridor. Orion turned to the left and began talking at the wall.

'As you can see, it is Orion,' the Cowboy drawled. 'Tell Ebanon I am here to see him as a matter of urgency.'

Nothing happened.

The General was just about to start shouting as to what the hell was happening, when all of a sudden the wall of the pitch black corridor that was illuminated only by Orion's belt, started to shimmer like it had turned into liquid.

'What you waiting for,' smiled Orion, and he walked through the shimmering wall and disappeared.

Isadora looked at Chinga. Chinga gulped. 'I'll go next' he said in a worried voice and slowly stepped through the shimmering black wall of the corridor.

'You next Miss Stone and I will bring up the rear,' barked the General.

Isadora looked at the shimmering wall, closed her eyes and stepped through it.

When she opened her eyes, she immediately had to put her hand up to her face to shield it from the light. The light in the room was blinding. As her eyes slowly adjusted, she saw that the room was huge. Due to the amount of equipment and the layout of the room, it appeared to be some sort of a laboratory. There were hundreds of small Greys, all in lines up and down the tables conducting some sort of experiments. At least that's what Isadora thought they were doing. Right at the back of the room, was a gigantic screen which appeared to show a picture of the night sky. What Isadora did not realise was this was a map of their homeland, Zeta Reticuli. Scattered around the room were some taller beings that looked like the smaller ones but were about 8 feet tall. They appeared to be over seeing what the little ones were doing. They were tall but nowhere near as tall as those huge creatures that had been on Chinga's planet, Isadora shuddered.

Isadora looked at Orion, what happens now she thought?

Now I request a meeting with Ebanon, Orion thought back.

Suddenly Isadora was aware of a large presence to the left of her. She snapped her head to the left to see who or what it was.

Walking towards her was a *towering* tall Grey. He looked different to the others who were working on their experiments and the taller ones who were over seeing them. The small Greys had not even looked up from their work as their party had walked in through the wall. Yet this tall Grey stared at them all quizzically. He must have been at least 10 feet tall Isadora thought. And he was really, really skinny with huge black, almond shaped eyes. A small nose and a little chin.

Suddenly Isadora heard a new voice in her head.

'Why are you here unannounced Orion, and why have you brought these *surface humans* and this other being with you?'

The huge tall grey stared at Chinga.

Isadora thought 'surface humans?' What did the tall grey alien mean?

Orion telepathically spoke to the immense alien.

'I apologise for just turning up here today Ebanon, but something has happened and I really need your help,' Orion explained.

'You need *my* help Orion,' scoffed Ebanon loudly. 'My, my, well let me see, how can I help?'

Isadora sensed that there was some history here between these two aliens, Orion being one of them.

'I know, it's a change for me to be asking for your help isn't it,' laughed Orion, and then his face fell serious. 'But I really do need your help Ebanon.'

'What can I help you with Orion,' said the huge tall being. Isadora was aware of a strange smell emanating from this creature. It was like the smell of mint and cinnamon and garbage, all rolled into one.

'My furry friend here,' Orion said gesturing to Chinga, 'has a problem. His planet has been attacked and taken over by some hideously, tall, *ugly* creatures. His family has been captured. We want to help him to take it back.'

'And you need my Technology to help you do this', Ebanon sneered, looking very happy that he was in this privileged position. That his Technology was so good that Orion needed it.

'Yes, Ebanon that's exactly what I need,' said Orion looking relieved that he didn't need to labour the point.

'Tell me more,' said Ebanon, whilst gesturing for the party to follow him somewhere. Ebanon started walking off into the distance with his long legs.

'So who is it that has 'taken' your planet?' Ebanon asked Chinga, turning round to look at him whilst still walking.

Chinga looked down at his feet and then back up at the tall alien.

'Valdazar' Chinga thought telepathically.

Ebanon's face changed instantly and he stopped in his tracks and turned around to face them all. 'Oh, oh, that changes everything,' he said in surprise. He turned around to speak to Orion. 'I'm sorry Orion. I can't help you.' Ebanon sounded like he was genuinely upset about this.

Orion looked at Ebanon and then back at Chinga whose face was devastated. 'Why, why can't you help us Ebanon?' The Cowboy asked. 'Chinga's family has been captured and his whole planet has been taken over!' He said incredulously.

'There is no way that I will stand against Valdazar, Orion.' The tall grey alien said gravely. 'I have let's say *an understanding* in place with him and the Valdons which goes back a long time, way before Valdazar himself took over the Valdons around 30 years ago. I cannot break this understanding. I am sorry I can't help you.'

Chinga fell to his knees with his head in his hands. Isadora knelt down to comfort him. General Myers looked on in disgust. It just occurred to Isadora that General Myers was the only one there who could not hear the conversation that was unfolding. As he couldn't speak telepathically he wouldn't have a clue what was going on.

'Is there anything that you can do to help us Ebanon? Just think of what I have done for you in the past when you needed help!' The Cowboy implored staring at him hard. Isadora could definitely tell that there was some interesting history between these two.

The giant alien looked pensive. 'Have you thought about the Agarthans?' Ebanon said. 'They have Technology too, very advanced. They could help you. They are of the light. There will be no understanding in place with Valdazar and them.'

Isadora thought that it looked as if Ebanon really wanted to help Orion, but for whatever reason he simply could not.

Orion pushed up his Cowboy hat and scratched his head. He had met with the Agarthans once in the past, but had never worked with them before. They kind of kept themselves to themselves and didn't mix with humans or aliens on the surface that much. Only when they needed something.

'Do you think they will help?' Orion asked the huge Grey.

'Why don't you ask them?' Ebanon said. 'I will bring the Ancient crystal and you can contact them?'

What's the Ancient crystal Isadora thought, and who on Earth are the Agarthans?

Orion looked at Isadora and said aloud for the benefit of the General. 'The Agarthans are some of the oldest beings on the planet. They are human, the original humans. They live deep inside the Earth in a City that they have created for themselves. In some of the Earth's natural, huge underground caverns. Orion continued. The Agarthans have lived inside Earth for 18 million years or thereabouts. They originally lived on the surface of the Earth but after witnessing and surviving several cataclysms on Earth, they decided the surface of the Earth was too risky a place to live, and they descended down into the natural caverns that exist within the Earth. Once they got down there, they created more space through their advanced Technology and bored out huge, vast rooms and cities under the surface of the planet.'

Orion had never seen them himself, but the cities of the Agarthans were supposed to be truly breath taking.

Ebanon turned and looked at Isadora with a quizzical look on his face. He was obviously wondering why a 15 year old girl was here with Orion on this mission. I must admit thought Isadora so am I!

'The Ancient crystals are a way that we underground beings have of contacting each other and other worlds,' Ebanon explained. 'Please wait here, I will fetch the crystal'. Ebanon suddenly disappeared with a 'pop' and then what seemed like seconds later, 'pop' he was back and holding a huge, pink crystal. He passed the crystal over to Orion.

Orion sat on the floor, cross-legged and put his hands on the crystal and closed his eyes. Isadora and Chinga copied Orion and sat on the floor next to him and watched. General Myers stood and scowled at Ebanon. Orion thought of the Agarthans and all of a sudden the crystal lit up and a beautiful, blonde woman appeared. Her stunning face was depicted inside the crystal. Isadora thought she was the most attractive woman she had ever seen. She had silver blond hair, huge crystal blue, almond shaped eyes, and a sleek heart shaped face. She looked human, but was the best looking human Isadora had ever seen. She had white robes on and a hood over her head.

'Hello Orion,' the woman purred, smiling at the huge Cowboy alien.

Orion blushed, 'Ah how do Ma-am. You know my name. Wow I didn't expect that?' The Cowboy laughed. For once he looks tongue tied Isadora thought. This could be interesting. Orion flashed a glance at Isadora and laughed. 'Ah yeah, I'm sorry, I don't know your name,' Orion said. 'You are obviously a member of the Agarthans?'

'Yes, I know who you are Orion,' said the beautiful woman. 'My name is Kaia. I am a priestess of the Agarthans. How can I help you?'

'Ah OK,' Orion said collecting his thoughts. 'My friend Chinga here lives on a planet called Delavia,' Orion began.

'The home of the famed Delavian Honey,' Kaia interjected with a smile.

'Yes that's right!' Said Chinga. 'You've heard of our Honey?' He said with a huge smile splitting across his face. That is the first time I have seen Chinga smile since we left Delavia Isadora thought.

'Of course said Kaia, who hasn't?' she said with a chuckle.

Isadora was starting to realise just how behind the curve humans were. Or as she realised today, *surface humans.* We weren't even just humans, we were known to everyone as *surface humans.* Not only were the American government working with Aliens at Area 51, but there were 'Greys' living on our planet under the Earth. And now there were Ancient humans living *inside* our planet? She sighed and rubbed her head. It was all too much for one day. What time had they got up that morning? 5am? And in that time they had been to Delavia, another world, been chased off by hideous creatures, come back and gone on a secret underground subway, had spoken to Grey aliens and now at 3pm they were talking to humans that lived inside the Earth through a magic crystal? Am I going insane she thought? Is this all a dream and I am still in bed? I hope not she suddenly thought as that meant that Momma would still be ill. Isadora's heart started to pound faster and her chest felt tight.

Orion hearing all this in Isadora's head turned and grabbed hold of her hands. 'Sorry Isadora I know this is a lot to take in for you. Are you OK? Are you OK to come with us or do you need me to take you back home to your Momma?' He said with great concern in his voice.

'No I'm fine,' Isadora reassured. 'I....it's just a lot to take in for one day. To learn that we humans are not alone. Not only that but aliens are living on our planet. And now we're talking to an Ancient human who lives inside our Earth. Sorry, I mean Kaia.'

'That's fine Isadora, it is nice to meet you,' Kaia said with a wise and sympathetic smile on her face. 'Why have you contacted me today Isadora and Orion. What is it that you want of the Agarthans?' The beautiful priestess asked politely.

'Ah, yes, OK,' Orion continued. 'As I was saying my friend Chinga lives on Delavia. He came to ask for our help as his kind, on his planet were getting sick. Real sick from eating the Honey from Earth. So we sent a party through a portal to Delavia with the purpose of visiting his kind and doing some tests and finding out was what was wrong, and hopefully healing them. We have our scientists currently working on finding out what has changed with Earth Honey and why it is effecting Chinga's kind the way it is.'

'Well I can tell you why that is happening,' Kaia interrupted Orion from telling his story.

'You can?' Chinga jumped in looking surprised. 'Why?'

'Your kind are getting sick Chinga, as Earth is becoming polluted and it is effecting the Honey. And I don't just mean pollution from the surface humans plastics and means of transport across the skies. The Honey is becoming polluted due to the negativity of mankind. The flowers are delicate beings that have consciousness of their own. They are absorbing all the negativity from surface humanity and this is effecting the nectar they produce. Which in turn is spoiling the Honey. You will not be able to eat the Honey from Earth Chinga until the surface humans have begun to work together instead of against each other. Until racial hatred and war has been replaced by humanity all working together towards a common cause. Namely their survival,' Kaia sighed.

Isadora and Chinga looked at each other in surprise. So the Honey was making Chinga's kind sick because the flowers that the bee's collected nectar from, were being effected by the negativity on Earth? That seemed a little farfetched?

Kaia directed her gaze at Isadora and continued. 'You surface humans will be next. You are able to tolerate a lot higher dose of negativity as you are subjected to it on a daily basis. You are not as delicate and as pure as Chinga's kind. But sometime soon, you surface humans will start to notice the effects of your own actions rain down upon yourselves. Soon the foods that you grow and eat that are grown in the ground. And the water that you drink that falls from the skies. Both of these things will start to make you sick. It will be a mess of your own making and Karma playing out full circle. You cannot expect to live the way you do, with no respect for the planet what so ever, and there be no negative effects to come back on surface humanity. Everything that you give out, always comes back to you. Our Earth is alive as well as you and I are, and she is effected by your negativity.' Kaia delivered all this harrowing news in such a sweet way that it was difficult to feel miffed with her.

It sounded like they were all doomed Isadora thought sarcastically. We're not all that bad she thought. But she had to admit, Kaia had a point. We don't look after our planet. She had seen the Blue Whale on the news which was made out of the plastic that was pulled out of the ocean in one second. One second only and this whale was huge. She had heard about the huge expanses of plastic that had all bonded together in the middle of the ocean around the Caribbean. We were chopping down the rain forests. We were pumping sewage into our oceans. The list of negative things that we were doing to our planet was endless. Isadora looked inside herself and felt sad. She must try and do more to make sure that she herself was not harming the planet. Her mind flicked back to when she threw her soup can in the 'normal' bin the other day instead of the one for recycling. She had done this as the other one was full. She felt shame in the pit of her stomach.

'OK, so it sounds like we may have worked out why Chinga's kind are getting sick,' Orion laughed trying to lighten the mood. 'I will make sure that information is relayed back to the powers that be and see if we can't clean up the planet.' He laughed as he knew that was likely impossible. Surface humans would not be happy until they had destroyed Earth. 'But the real reason that we have contacted you today is because we need your help. When we landed on Delavia in order to find out what was going on with Chinga's kind. We quickly realised that the planet had been taken over whilst Chinga was over on Earth negotiating with us. It's a real nasty guy called Valdazar. He is the leader of the Valdons from planet Valdar which is a planet in the next Galaxy over from ours. He has taken the planet. We can only assume that he has done this in order to acquire the Delavian Honey for trade.' Orion continued after taking a huge breath. 'We have contacted you as we were hoping that you would help us take the planet back. We need your ships.' Orion finished.

'I see,' said Kaia. She looked troubled. 'I also see that you have contacted me from Ebanon's crystal. So the Agarthans were not your first choice of help?'

Orion went red and fumbled with his belt. 'Yes, we came to see Ebanon first as he is an old acquaintance of mine who owes me a favour,' Orion said pointedly. 'But it appears that he will not help us out on this one. He has some sort of agreement in place with Valdazar and because of that he cannot help us.'

'Doesn't want to help you more like,' said Kaia. 'Valdazar is not someone to be messed with.'

Isadora could see where this was going.

'I am not sure that the Agarthans will want to get involved in this. However as you have contacted me via the crystal for our help, I must put this to our council for a group decision,' Kaia continued.' I must ask that you come to the City of Agartha to discuss this personally with the council,' Kaia finished.

Orion looked at Chinga and Isadora, 'Well what do you think?' said Orion.

'Yes we need to go,' said Chinga. 'We have to save my people and Delavia.'

'Yes lets go!' Said Isadora. Today couldn't get much crazier she thought.

Orion looked finally at the General who was as always frowning. 'Where is this Agartha City soldier so I can inform our troops where we are going?' Barked the General.

I don't know said Orion, but it looks like we are about to find out.

Trade

Valdazar was bored. How much longer would he be made to wait? This made him angry. Nobody makes *Valdazar* wait he thought. It was a sign of disrespect. And he *hated* being disrespected. He was waiting for the merchant race which he traded with to turn up with his new ship, in return for the first instalment of Delavian Honey. The first of many he smiled and rubbed his hands.

He had resorted to throwing rocks at the Ancient ones and seeing if he could make them jump. So far they seemed incapable of jumping, no matter how hard he pelted the rocks at the fat, flabby, creatures. All they did was wince. It looked like they'd even lost the ability to speak normally over time. As they could only speak telepathically through Valdazar's slave. Although you still have mouths don't you, you vile things he thought. As otherwise how else would you have gotten so fat other than stuffing your faces? He currently had one of the smaller furry things that he assumed was a child. Finding new rocks for him to throw, as he had run out. He was taking his time bringing back more. He had better not run off, Valdazar thought angrily. Just as he was about to send some of the huge Valdons off to find the little furry thing, it came running back with more rocks. 'Good furry thing,' Valdazar sneered as he took a rock from him. 'Can you talk?' said Valdazar to the Sasquatch child.

The small creature looked up at Valdazar, 'Yes, I can', he said quietly looking back at his feet. 'What is your name creature?' Valdazar asked. The Sasquatch child looked up into Valdazar's face, holding his chin high.

'My name is Peets,' he said defiantly. 'Well *Peets*,' sneered Valdazar. Let's see how good your aim is. Ten points for one of their faces and if you get it on the nose, twenty points, he laughed as he resumed throwing rocks at the Ancients.

The Great City of Agartha

Ebanon the head Grey had led the party into a room within his sprawling underground complex, which had a Technological portal in it. This was, Orion explained like the portal that the party had gone through earlier in the day when they had travelled to Delavia. But instead of being natural, it was man made. So to speak, Isadora thought and smiled to herself.

Isadora stared at the portal. As it was not a natural portal, this one was a large, silver metal ring that looked like a horseshoe. Presumably you stepped into it to portal out. It was large, at least 15 feet tall. But then it would need to be for the Greys to use it. Ebanon himself was very tall indeed.

'Thanks for your help Ebanon,' Orion said telepathically to the huge Grey.

'I am only sorry that I could not help more, but as you know, I cannot break an understanding,' Ebanon replied.

'Yes of course, reassured Orion. I get it.'

Ebanon looked at Isadora and realised from the expression on her face that she was very apprehensive about stepping into the portal.

'Do not worry surface human,' the large Grey Alien said. 'Just follow Orion into the portal and it will take you where you want to go. Orion it has been good to see you. Until next time.'

Orion looked at Isadora and the rest of his party. 'Until next time my friend,' Orion said smiling at the huge grey alien. 'Yes, Ebanon is right, just follow me into the portal and in the blink of an eye we will be in Agartha.'

Orion shot Isadora a dazzling smile and stepped forward into the portal and disappeared.

'You next Isadora,' said Chinga and gestured for her to step forwards.

Isadora steeled herself, took a deep breath and stepped in. This time, she felt the huge hard pull like thousands of strings pulling her through. But it wasn't as jolty or traumatic and when she opened her eyes, she did not feel sick at all. She stepped to the side to let her companions come through and surveyed the scene in front of her in amazement.

She was in a *gigantic* cave. It was massive. She could see it was a cave from the wall which was nearest to her. But as she squinted, she definitely could not see where the cave ended. It seemed to go on forever. It was beautiful. It was a perfect mixture of modern and traditional. Futuristic and nature. Stretching out in front of her were rolling hills, trees, lush grass and rivers. There were also fields and fields of plants or crops as far as the eye could see. There were exotic birds flying around overhead. And the sights, sounds and smells of nature all around. Yet above all this, were flying disks, zipping around the sky on what looked to be some kind of sky highway. Isadora watched one of the disks fly past her and was astonished when it was heading straight for the cave wall nearest to her.

'Orion! She said panicked, that disk is heading straight for the cave wall! It looks like it's about to *hit*.....' She screamed the last part and ducked her head under her hands as she braced for impact. But nothing happened. No sound, no blinding lights, no crash, nothing. When Isadora looked up, she saw that *all* the disks were whizzing past her and directly i*nto* the cave wall. How on Earth? She thought. Or should I say, how *in* Earth, Isadora laughed to herself. These disks were somehow flying through the cave wall like it wasn't even there. When Isadora stopped gawping at the disks and looked down, she saw that Orion was stood about 20 paces away from their group talking to the beautiful, blonde woman called Kaia. Isadora was shocked as to how tall she was. Orion himself was really tall, probably about 8 feet tall. But Kaia was only slightly smaller than him. Orion was nodding, he stepped away from Kaia and returned back to his party.

'Right,' said the huge Cowboy. 'Kaia has organised a council meeting for us, to discuss whether they are willing to help us. It goes without saying that we really, really need them to help us. So please do all that you can to make this happen. I will lead negotiations as usual but Chinga I will need your help to convince them given that Delavia is your planet.'

'Yes of course,' said Chinga. 'I will do all that I can to convince them to help my people, and my family.' Chinga looked at the floor his eyes filling with tears.

General Myers rolled his eyes and snorted. 'Come on, let's get this over with Cowboy so we can get on with the war. I have ground troops on standby waiting for my direction soldier.'

'Ah and there's one more thing' said Orion looking sheepish. Nobody spoke, everyone was waiting to see what he was going to say. 'Ah, we have to be cleansed before they will let us into the council meeting.'

'*Cleansed*,' sneered General Myers. 'What do you mean soldier?'

'Ah, I'm not entirely sure,' said Orion going red. 'But I think it involves us getting naked.'

'You're joking right?' said Isadora incredulously.

'Ah no, I'm not joking, we need to be clean of the surface before we can enter their holy place, which is where the council meeting is being held.'

Chinga laughed his head off, a huge belly laugh. 'Well I'm fine with that!' He giggled running his hand over his fur.

'You're already naked creature!' Sneered General Myers. 'There's no way I'm taking off my skivvies not here not ever. That is *not* part of the mission,' he said angrily.

'Ah, I would appear that it is,' said Orion as Kaia began walking towards them.

'Are you ready for the cleansing process my friends?' The beautiful priestess asked.

'Yes' said Orion and Chinga in unison. 'Errr, I guess?' said Isadora thinking there was no way in hell she was getting naked in front of Orion. 'Is there a separate one for males and females asked Isadora embarrassed?

Kaia looked at Isadora. 'Ah yes, I forgot that you surface humans are embarrassed by your own bodies. If it would make you feel more comfortable Isadora then you can cleanse first and then the rest of your party can go in after.'

'Plus there's laws to abide by here. This girl is technically still a minor in our world. We can't be showering with her!' Barked the General sarcastically.

'You will not be showering General,' said Kaia with a smile. 'You will be cleansing.'

'I won't be doing anything that involves me taking my uniform off soldier.' Stated the General with bluster.

'Then I am truly sorry,' said Kaia looking genuinely upset. 'But I cannot permit you to enter our City. You must take the portal back to whence you have come.'

General Myers went every shade of crimson and then just admitted defeat realising that there was no way out of this one. 'Lead the way soldier,' he barked.

Orion looked at Isadora, 'OK then lets follow Kaia.'

They all turned and started to follow the tall, blonde woman through the huge, immense cavern.

The Merchants

'You're doing well Peets,' Valdazar laughed encouraging the small Sasquatch. 'Throw more, try and aim for their faces!' He squealed.

Peets had actually not even thrown one rock yet. He could not, would not throw rocks at the Ancients. As much as the Ancients were selfish creatures who ruled Delavia in a strict manner keeping all of the Honey for themselves. They were still the rulers of his planet, and he would not throw rocks. This crazy man was having so much fun pelting the Ancients himself that he didn't seem to realise that Peets had not even thrown one rock.

Until now.

Valdazar was laughing so hard having just managed to hit the really fat one straight on the nose. 'Peets, you've stopped throwing! Throw another one, I'm winning!' He laughed.

'No', said Peets.

Valdazar stopped laughing and turned to face the small Sasquatch. This small furry thing had a lot of confidence for someone whose planet had just been over thrown.

'What did you say to me?' Valdazar said in a low dangerous voice. He was half astonished that this creature could be so brave and half angry.

'I said No!' Said Peets raising his voice. 'I will not throw rocks at my people!'

Valdazar was just about to pick the little furry thing up and throw *it* at the Ancients, when a huge Valdon lumbered in as quickly as it could.

'They are here Sire,' the Valdon informed.

'Excellent!' said Valdazar. Seemingly forgetting Peets straight away. 'Bring them in'. He ran and climbed onto his throne. He wanted to look all powerful when they came in.

Peets seized the moment and ran off into the darkness. In Valdazar's haste to get to his throne. He did not see this happening. All Valdazar was thinking about was receiving the merchants and obtaining his new ship. And the huge Valdon had left to bring in the guests. *No-one* saw Peets escape other than the Ancients themselves.

Peets looked back once as he escaped to check he was not being followed. And he ran off into the darkness.

The merchants were brought before Valdazar. They were tall, very tall. With humanoid bodies and their heads looked like the heads of Doberman dogs.

'Anubis!' Shouted Valdazar. 'So good to see you my friend! As you can see, I have the Honey that you require.' Valdazar was so happy, and smug. He couldn't wait to see his new ship.

'As I can see Valdazar,' laughed Anubis the leader of the merchants. 'How did you manage to conquer this planet? Those things are pretty big?' Anubis pointed at the fat Ancients who were currently rubbing their bruised bits from Valdazar's earlier pummeling.

'It was a lot easier than you might think Anubis. Especially when you are me!' Valdazar laughed.

'Quite,' said Anubis in a tone that acknowledged Valdazar's ability to brutally conquer a planet when required.

'So where is my Honey?' The huge dog like creature asked.

'So where is my ship?' Valdazar sneered.

'I thought you might ask that,' Anubis said laughing. 'Look up'

Valdazar looked up at the night sky. Just as a huge ship appeared directly above where they were stood.

'I had it cloaked,the large dog said. I wanted to make sure that you really had the Honey first. Before I hand over the ship.'

'I am a man of my word am I not?' Valdazar laughed.

'When it suits,' thought Anubis. Valdazar obviously couldn't hear this as he was not telepathic. Something which really, really annoyed

Valdazar. He hated any form of weakness and here was an area where he was weak. Where others were strong. 'Of course you are Valdazar' Anubis said aloud. Directly contradicting what he had just thought.

'Your first instalment of Honey is there crated up.' Valdazar pointed to a huge pile of Honey pots that had been placed inside a makeshift crate that had obviously been whittled out of the trees on Delavia. It looked very authentic. Valdazar was quite pleased with himself.

Anubis frowned. 'No expense spared on the packaging.' He thought. But aloud he said 'Very rustic looking Valdazar, excellent.' He turned to beckon his henchmen to start loading the Honey onto their own ship. He turned back to Valdazar, 'It's been a pleasure doing business with you as usual Valdazar, Anubis smiled. *And now to get out of your rancid presence.'* He thought through gritted teeth.

Human stood in the shadows behind his master's throne and listened to everything that was unfolding. Of course he could hear everything that Anubis was thinking as well as saying. It was obvious that Anubis only tolerated his master as they had a pretty good business relationship. But Anubis obviously hated Valdazar. Human saw this time and time again. The beings who spoke to Valdazar looked like they were in awe of him and respected him. They all said the right things and paid homage where they needed to. But really *everyone* thought he was a joke. They all thought he was a joke as *he was a human.* A human of Earth, and everyone in the Cosmos knew just how stupid humans were. They were slaves to their leaders. Slaves to money. Slaves to the 'rat race'. Slaves to their hatred of each other. Constantly blowing each other up in the name of religion and allowing small children to starve and die of diseases that they had the capability to treat.

Everyone across the Cosmos thought humans were foolish and blinkered. They did not look after their own. It was obvious time and time again that there was other life out in the Universe. But the humans just chose to ignore this. Like ostriches with their heads in the sand. Various races had allowed themselves to be seen by the human race yet their leaders had laughed these occurrences off as weather balloons or 'new craft' that the United States had. The best one was 'Swamp Gas'.

The Pleiadians and Arcturians had been leaving intricate crop circles for years with images that no human could ever have created. Yet humans still believed that their people in power had not yet found intelligent life elsewhere in the vast Cosmos. They had managed to convince them that 'humans made the crop circles with sticks'. Of course the real people in power on the Earth, the shadow government were *fully aware* of the existence of aliens and had been working alongside them, across space since the 20's. Hell some of them even had seats on the Super Alliance Councils. Yet there was *no way* that they were going to let the average human know this. They would do *anything* to hold onto their privileged position of power. If they did let the average Joe know about the existence of life elsewhere in the Cosmos, and allow them to see what Technology other beings had which don't require gas, petrol, money etc. Then they would lose their monopolies on oil, and cars and gas. If humans found out that there was free energy and they didn't need to be burning fossil fuels. If they knew that there was Technology called 'Replicators' which cooked you any meal you wanted. If they knew there were natural portals and technological portals on Earth which could transport you wherever you wanted to go throughout the Cosmos. What would they think? What would they do? But it didn't matter thought Human as all these things were being kept from the average human. Why lose control of the slaves when you can manipulate them to do whatever you want he thought bitterly. The rich people of the world wanted to get richer and maintain control. The only way to do that is to keep the average human believing that they were the only life out there in the entire Universe. What would humans think thought 'Human' if they knew that people were dying of diseases that *they* already had the Technology to cure? That children were dying all over Earth from starvation. When the shadow government already had the Technology to feed them with whatever they wanted, every day, for the rest of their lives? And that the shadow government is already out here in the Universe, flying around in Technology equally as good as the average alien has! But the average human on Earth has no idea. It is kept secret. 'The secrets I would be able to divulge if I ever manage to make it home to Earth,' Human thought sadly. I just need to bide my time he thought. At some point someone will come along who can help me get out of here. Just hang in there. Stay alert. An opportunity will present itself at some point. I just need to keep my eyes and ears open.

As Human watched Anubis leave and another opportunity to escape the clutches of his master disappeared. He felt sadder and lonelier than ever.

'Human!' Shouted Valdazar. 'It is time for us to try out our new ship and leave this place. Arrange for twenty of the Valdons to stay here in order to ensure these creatures don't break out and escape, and also to keep collecting the Honey. The rest are to come with us on the new ship. I will meet you on the new ship in ten minutes.' He shouted whilst stalking away to check out his new toy.

'Yes Sire,' responded Human and he set about completing his master's instructions.

Cleansing

The cleansing process was something that Isadora did not want to repeat anytime soon. It's not very often you go to a new place under the surface of the Earth's crust and then have to get naked the first five minutes of being there. Thankfully Kaia had kept to her word and let her 'cleanse' separately. She thought the fact that she was technically still a minor helped this decision. As otherwise for speed she would have been lumped in with the rest of them.

Cleansing consisted of being led into a huge beautiful cavern that had a natural waterfall cascading down into a huge natural rock pool. However the water was the colour of milk. In the middle was a statue of a beautiful female goddess. This statue had obviously been stood there for a very long time as it was covered in mineral deposits from the water and had built up quite a crust on it. Isadora didn't get chance to ask Kaia who this beautiful lady immortalised in stone was, as she was concentrating on getting her clothes off and washing in the freezing cold pool as quickly as possible. She was told by Kaia when quickly splashing freezing cold water over her goose pimply body, that she was to put on the robes that had been left out for her. Her 'surface' clothes would be returned to her when she left Agartha.

When Isadora had finished washing her body and could no longer bear the cold. She turned round to check no one was watching and jumped out of the pool. The robes were suspended in the air as if by an invisible coat hanger. Isadora tentatively plucked them out of the air and put them on as quickly as possible. They were white and very comfortable. They were made out of a material that instantly took the chill away that Isadora had been feeling and made her feel 'just right'. In fact she could see that she was wearing the robes on her body, but the weight of the fabric was so light that she was not encumbered by it at all.

What now? She thought. 'Ah I'm finished!' Shouted Isadora into the darkness of the dimly lit cavern. Kaia stepped out of the shadows. 'Excellent, I will now bring your friends in to repeat the process.' And she left the cave.

In what seemed like seconds later. In walked Kaia with Orion, Chinga and General Myers.

Orion was already half naked. Seemingly he couldn't wait to jump in this freezing cold pool. Chinga was laughing under his breath at the obvious discomfort of General Myers. General Myers' face was bright red and she could see a little muscle ticking in his jaw.

'Let's get this over with soldier!' Barked The General.

Kaia led Isadora out of the cavern and into the light.

As Isadora walked out of the cave she heard Orion shout

'Last one in's a chicken!'

Isadora laughed.

Update

The President had been waiting all afternoon for an update. What was happening? And what did he do with this new information that had been dropped on him today. Grey Aliens had a base on Earth. Not just on Earth but in Dulce, New Mexico. *In America*! His America. What did he do with that?

Suddenly the phone rang. He jumped and answered it straight away.

'This is The President.' He said down the phone.

The same operative began speaking.

'Ah Sir, we have no update.'

'What do you mean?' He said in exasperation.

'Well we traced them to the Greys underground base in Dulce, New Mexico Sir. Since then, they haven't come out. We don't know what they are doing in there Sir. Or if in fact they are even still in there. They could have left by other means.'

'Other means?' Exclaimed The President quizzically. 'How else could they have left this base other than by the way they came in?' He didn't understand.

'They could have left via spaceship Sir. Or via a technological portal.' The monotone voice informed.

'Spaceship?' The President exclaimed. 'They have spaceships underground?'

'Yes Sir they do', said the operative.

'Do you have anything else to tell me at this time?' The President said impatiently. He had been waiting what seemed like forever for this update and the operative hadn't really updated him at all.

'Not at this time Sir.' The operative confirmed.

'Call me when you do.' He said slamming down the phone.

Where were they? And what were they doing?

The Agarthans Council Meeting

Kaia had led Orion, Isadora, Chinga and General Myers from the cleansing room into another much smaller cavern. It had a huge, stone table in it. Much like a table that you get in conference rooms on Earth. It was obviously very old and was whittled out of a grey stone. Around the table sat about twenty members of the Agarthans. Some had robes on like they were now currently wearing. Some had more normal looking clothes. As in they wore trousers and tops and dresses which looked to have been fashioned out of really expensive materials. Their clothes were very ornate in all different bold colours. Fashioned out of materials that looked like silk. Isadora also noticed that all of these people were wearing pendants around their necks which looked to be in the shape of a spiral. She looked at Kaia and she also was wearing the same pendant. Had she always had that on Isadora wondered or am I just noticing it now?

All eyes were on the party of four and she could see all of these Ancient humans studying them up and down. I wonder when the last time was that they saw anyone from surface Earth she thought? She saw a lot of the people round the table were taking a particular interest in her. She had no idea why given there was a huge Sasquatch stood next to her and an 8 foot tall Cowboy. Isadora noticed pretty quickly that all of the people round the table were very good looking and nobody seemed to be old. They all looked in their twenties? Where were all the old people?

'Please take a seat at the table.' Gestured Kaia and the party of four sat down at the large, stone table.

Slowly silence filtered around the room.

Kaia spoke first, 'Orion, Isadora, Chinga and General Myers contacted me earlier today to ask for our help.' Kaia spoke into the silent room. The sound of her voice echoed around the cavern.

'Chinga is from Delavia. His planet has been taken over by Valdazar of the Valdons and they have come to ask for our help and our ships in order to take it back.'

The room stayed silent.

Isadora looked from face to face. No-one's face had changed. They all looked like they were still waiting for Kaia to carry on and say something else.

Finally, someone spoke. A man. He had beautiful bright blond hair like Kaia and attractive features. He was not dressed in robes like Kaia but had what looked like warrior type clothes on, albeit still in silk material. Isadora wondered whether he was a soldier in their society.

'Why should we help this Chinga?' The man asked the group. 'Delavia is in another Solar system to the one we are in here. Valdazar does not have a quarrel with us. Why should we highlight him to our existence?'

'Yes,' said another man further down the table who was equally as attractive. 'Hyperion is right. We have lived within the Earth for millions of years and we do not get involved with other people's wars. We don't even get involved in the wars of surface humans who live **on** Earth. Why would we get involved with a war which has nothing to do with us at all?' The second man asked the table.

Chinga was watching this unfold and getting more and more upset. The thought of his family being captured by Valdazar and him not being able to help them was too much to bare. He jumped up and addressed the table. All eyes looked at him in shock as he started speaking.

'Please I beg you, help me. Help Delavia. Help my family. I have two children. A little boy called Peets and a little girl called Sneets. Peets is a wonderfully curious little thing and he is already making me proud every day in how quick he learns things. His Sister is the same. They are both so curious and inquisitive. They are happy, bright, shining, souls. Always happy. They are the light in my life. I wasn't there to protect them when they needed me the most. I let them down. *Please* don't let Valdazar take my children away and sell them as slaves. I will never find them again. Please help me save my family. I beg you!' The huge furry creature began crying silently. Isadora's heart broke. Chinga had never spoken about his children before to her. This was the first time she had heard any details about them. Chinga was a Daddy. She had to help her friend.

Isadora stood up.

'This may not be your fight now. And I understand why you are reluctant to get involved with it. But Valdazar is showing a pattern here. He is slowly conquering planet after planet. He started in his own Solar system. Then moved throughout his own Galaxy. And now he has started in our Galaxy. This is the first planet within our Galaxy that he has 'taken'. If we stand back and do nothing. How long will it be before Valdazar decides to come here and 'take' Earth. Given that he is from here? Is it not better to show strength now, and show that our Galaxy will not be beaten and that we stand together. Before Valdazar turns the might of the Valdons on us?'

There was a buzz of whispering around the table. What this young lady had said was true and it was from the heart. But what was this she said about Valdazar being of Earth. If he was a human of Earth, it is true that his natural curiosity to return would be a normal thing. And given the type of person that he clearly was, he would surely want to return to Earth as a mighty conqueror and take over Earth too.

Everyone around the table started talking animatedly. 'He's a surface human!' Someone shouted. 'Of course he will come back here and conquer the Earth. We cannot let him do that!'

Kaia held up her hand and all at once everyone around the table stopped talking.

She looked at each one of the council individually. Isadora could tell that she was speaking to each one telepathically but that the party from the surface could not hear them. This was the first time that she had not been able to hear someone telepathically. Could Orion hear them? She wondered or Chinga? But from the look on their faces she could tell that they could not hear what was being said either.

Kaia said aloud, 'It is decided then. We will help you.'

There was a visible slump in Chinga's body as the tension that he had been holding released. He began crying with renewed vigour. General Myers scowled.

'However we have some conditions.' The beautiful woman said.

'Anything,' said Chinga, 'anything at all.'

Kaia smiled at Chinga. 'I am afraid Chinga that these conditions are not yours to grant.'

Chinga stopped crying and looked at Kaia.

'The conditions that we have concern your friend Isadora here.' Kaia continued.

All eyes at the table turned to Isadora. Isadora gulped. She hated being the centre of attention.

Kaia continued. 'We are conscious that our efforts to *help* surface humanity over time has not gone as well as we had hoped. Over the ages we have presented ourselves to surface humans and pretended to be gods, in order to try and educate and help them choose the right path. We have tried to impress upon them the importance of being kind to each other, helping each other and looking after the planet. But each time we have done that, the main message has been distorted into something else. And the true message lost. More recently we have changed our tactics and spoken to surface humans as 'aliens' and tried to get these same messages across. To look after the Earth. To look after each other. To treat each other with kindness no matter what colour of skin a person has or where they live on the planet. However the people we have targeted have been unable to change the population's mass consciousness. We had not wanted our location to become known to the surface humans as we feared for our safety. We thought if we were considered as gods or aliens that humans would always be looking to the skies for us, instead of under their feet. However we feel that times on the surface of Earth are changing and we have been thinking for a long time now about making ourselves known to the surface humans. We are waiting for the right time. We think that time will be soon. When that time becomes apparent. We would like Miss Stone here to represent us to the surface humans.'

Isadora had listened to all of this and had no idea what that meant. 'I'm sorry Kaia, I don't understand what you want me to do?' she said confused.

Kaia smiled. 'You don't need to do anything for the time being Isadora. But when the time comes. And we feel it is coming soon. We have seen the changes on Earth. When the time comes for our existence to be revealed on mass to the surface humans of the Earth. We want you to be our spokesperson. Who better to speak for us than a teenage American girl who is one of their people? Who has actually been here and witnessed our City for yourself. They will have to believe you. And they will know that they are safe and that we mean no harm. That we have always been here beneath their feet, waiting for the right time to make ourselves known. That we were actually here before they were.'

Isadora suddenly understood. 'You want me to be your representative? To our people? When the time comes.'

'Yes that is correct Isadora,' smiled Kaia.

'Yes' smiled Isadora. 'I would be happy to do that.'

Kaia smiled. 'We also believe Isadora that you are correct in what you say about Valdazar. If we do not act now, he will eventually move to our Solar system and attack Gaia. Gaia is the name that we

Agarthans use when we refer to the planet Earth. We need to show strength now. So it appears Miss Stone and Chinga that we have a deal. Now let's discuss how we help Chinga here take back his planet. And perhaps Chinga you might let us have some of your famed Delavian Honey in return. Once we have taken back your planet?' Kaia teased.

Chinga laughed, 'Kaia,' he smiled his huge toothy grin. 'You can have anything you want.'

Everyone laughed.

The New Spaceship

Valdazar was currently sat on his new spaceship laughing his head off.

'This thing is great!' He squealed. 'Look, I just think where I want to go, and it *goes* there!'

Human nodded, 'Yes Sire'.

'Where shall we go next Human?' Valdazar laughed.

Human so badly wanted to say Earth. He so badly wanted to go home. To see his family again. To see his wife and his daughter. It had been 4 years since he had been taken by the Valdons to work as Valdazar's telepath. I bet my daughter has grown up so much, Human thought sadly. But there is no way that Human would encourage Valdazar to go to Earth. Best he forgets that he was ever from there he thought. I never ever, ever want to see him turn the might of the Valdons onto my home planet. When Valdazar had originally said that they would be going to Delavia, Human had been both happy and scared at the same time. Happy as Delavia was in the same Galaxy as Earth and he was one step closer to getting home. And sad as he knew that if his master started focusing his attention on the Milky Way. Then that would mean eventually, he would conquer Earth and his wife and daughter would no doubt suffer the same fate as he had.

No, Human thought. Keep that monster as far away from my family as possible.

Human thought of a planet as far away from Earth as possible.

'How about Unatron Sire?' Human suggested.

'Excellent idea Human. We've not been there for a while. Let's go and see if the Unatrons are as annoying as they ever were!'

Valdazar put his hands on the steel plate at the front of the craft and thought of Unatron. Suddenly the screen at the front of the craft showed them Unatron. And a worm hole opened up in front of the craft.

'Hold onto your hat Human!' Laughed Valdazar. 'Here we go!'
And the craft hopped into the wormhole and disappeared from view.

The Scout

The Agarthans Council meeting had carried on a little while longer, and two additional things had been decided. Firstly that a scout was to be sent to Delavia that night to assess the lay of the land and to find out how many Valdons they were looking at defeating. Secondly, that a feast was to be held that night in honour of their new companions. It had been a very long time since they had had visitors from the surface as guests and the Agarthans wanted to show the *surface humans* what a civilised society they were.

The scout was to leave through the technological portal that the Agarthans had in their City that night. They would go to Delavia to see what was currently happening on the planet in order that they may best devise their plan of attack.

Chinga had begged Kaia for the Scout to check for his family whilst he was on Delavia. But this request had been denied.

Kaia had told Chinga that the scout literally had to go in and out and do a reconnaissance mission only. Alerting no one to his presence at all. He did not have time to converse with anyone and find Chinga's family. As if he was found he could potentially blow their cover and element of surprise. As soon as the planet was re-taken the following day. They would look for Chinga's family as a matter of urgency.

Chinga whilst upset obviously understood the logic of this.

The meeting then closed with Kaia explaining that as they wouldn't be leaving for Delavia until the morning, a feast would be held in their honour that night. They were now to be escorted to their sleeping quarters for the night to get ready for the feast and clothes would be provided to them for the occasion.

As they filed out of the council meeting into the open courtyard outside, Kaia beckoned to a tall, dark haired man. All of the Agarthans that Isadora had met so far had whitish, blond hair and she was somewhat surprised to see that some of the Agarthans had very dark hair.

'Tiamut,' shouted Kaia to the tall dark haired man. 'Please can you escort Isadora to the first of the guest rooms that we have? She will be staying with us here tonight. I must get back to the temple.'

'Yes Kaia, of course' said Tiamut in a knowing voice. He turned to greet Isadora. 'Hello Isadora, I am Tiamut. I am one of the elders here in Agartha City.'

Elders? Thought Isadora, he only looked about 40 years old. If that?

'Hi Tiamut,' smiled Isadora. 'I am Isadora Stone and I'm errr, a surface human.' *Apparently,* she said under her breath.

'I am pleased to make your acquaintance said the large dark haired man. Allow me to escort you to your sleeping quarters for tonight.' And the two strode off into the unparalleled beauty which was Agartha City.

Peets

Peets had watched from the shadows behind a tree as Valdazar and most of the Valdon Army left in their new ship. He *hated* that man. He had then waited until it had got dark and snuck back into the camp. He had to find his Mother and Sister and get them out. And if he could, he intended to free all of his people. Now that Valdazar had gone, they might have some of a chance of defeating the remaining Valdons. If he could get all of his people out.

The problem was that a lot of them particularly the males, were sick. He wondered if it had something to do with the tradition of Honey fetching as it was only the males who did this. His thoughts went to his Father Chinga. He had seen him leave the planet two nights before. He had followed him quietly and watched him walk through the shimmering bubble. He so wanted to go with him. He had often asked his Father if he could accompany him to the Honey giving planet. But Father had told him that he was too young yet.

He was so looking forward to fetching Honey with his dad when he was older. He had no idea if his Father had come back yet. Surely if he had, he would have tried to save them by now? He was worried about his Father, really worried. But as he didn't know where he was, there was nothing he could do about him yet. But he *could* do something to save his Mother and his Sister. He took a deep breath and crept out from the darkness.

The Feast

Tiamut had proved to be a wonderful companion on the journey to Isadora's sleeping quarters for the night. He had filled her in a bit about the Agarthans. It seemed that there was no money in their society which shocked Isadora immensely. She couldn't imagine how Americans would feel without having money. It was the American Dream right? Tiamut had explained that money was how a society was controlled, and the Agarthans did not control their people. All their people were treated as equal. Apparently when you have money in place, this keeps the population enslaved. As they constantly need to go out to earn the money to pay for their lives. Isadora certainly thought that most people she knew would agree with that. Who wanted to wake up on a Monday morning and go to work?

Tiamut had explained that at Agartha City, everything that they had was shared between the people. Everyone in their City had access to their super Technology. Which included state of the art spaceships. No-one was ever sick as the Agarthans had the Technology to heal anything and they knew how to look after their bodies. Although they had Technology which allowed them to eat anything they wanted, whenever they wanted. They preferred to grow their own crops and food sources underground, following a high vibration diet. They didn't eat meat of any kind. They did eat fish occasionally which lived in the underground lakes. But they preferred to follow a high vegetable content diet. This turned Isadora's stomach a bit, she could not image life without meat. She loved barbeque food and pit plates and pulled pork and smoked bacon. Although she did feel guilty that all of these yummy things came from animals. As she loved animals. Tiamut was just explaining when they reached her room that they obtained anything that they needed for their people by trading the organic fruit and vegetables that they grew underground. Apparently throughout the Cosmos, the Agarthan fruit and vegetables were famed much as Delavian Honey was.

'And here we are Isadora,' said Tiamut as they had apparently reached Isadora's sleeping quarters. 'I will give you an hour to freshen up and change and then I will come back and pick you up for the feast.' Tiamut said smiling.

Isadora noticed that there was no lock on her door. Tiamut did not unlock the door to her room. He simply opened the door. Jeez that's weird. I really hope no one just walks in on me whilst I'm getting changed thought Isadora shivering. She walked inside her room and her jaw dropped in awe. It was built out of the rock underground and the ceilings were much lower than in the main cavern and the meeting room that they had been in.

She bade goodbye to Tiamut and entered her room.

It was breath taking. There was a huge white bed at the end of the room up against the rock face. And all around the room were lit candles. They created shadows on the rock walls and gave the room a very romantic feel. She walked up to the bed as something caught her eye on there. She realised that the red garment laid out on her bed was her feast outfit. That was pretty breath taking too. It was in the ornate style of the Agarthans and was sort of a red silk pantsuit. On the pantsuit in the top left corner was the same symbol that she had noticed on the pendants of the Agarthans Council. It was a small silver spiral that looked much like the spiral of a Galaxy.

So where does someone get a shower in this place Isadora thought and all of a sudden in the corner of the room, hot steaming water started to fall. It poured straight down into a rock pool that contained the water underneath.

Wow thought Isadora, this place is incredible.

The Great Escape

Peets had slowly circled the entire camp and had seen where his people were being held. Most of them had fallen to sleep now. He hoped he would be able to wake them up without alerting the Valdons. He had tried really hard to see if he could see his Mother and Sister Sneets. But he had not been able to locate them in the pen so far. An anxious feeling filled his little chest. They must be in there. It looked like the Valdons had rounded up most if not all of their people. All except Father of course. His thoughts turned to his Father. Had he come back already from the Honey planet? He couldn't have done. If he had, he would have tried to save everyone. Much like he was going to do now. Father is a good person thought Peets. He would always try to do what is right.

When Valdazar and the Valdons had arrived he had not been with his Mother and Sister. He had been out in the woods waiting for his Father to return from the Honey planet. He had followed him on the night he had left and seen him walk into the shimmery, wavy bubble and disappear. His Father would have been mad with him if he had known what he was doing. Father had said he would take him with him when he was older but that he was not old enough yet. But what Father did not yet realise, thought Peets. Is that I *am* old enough. I am old enough to go to the Honey Planet and I'm old enough to save my people. He was a bit embarrassed that he had been caught by the Valdons in the end. He was creeping back to the camp to see what all the noise was when he had seen them. He had been so scared worrying about his Mother and Sister. Whilst he had been watching the drama unfold in the camp. Two Valdons who had been out in the forest looking for stragglers had caught him and brought him before Valdazar. As he had been small, and they obviously did not see him as a threat. They had never chucked him in the pen with the rest of his people. They had kept him out and used him to run errands for them. As he was smaller and quicker. And with Delavia being his planet. He knew where things were. He had spent a long time looking for rocks for Valdazar.

He looked over at the huge disgusting Valdons and counted that there were twenty left on Delavia. The rest had gone in the new ship with Valdazar and left. All of these remaining Valdons were currently sat round a camp fire. Ripping into smoking cooked carcasses of large animals. They had been roasting these anomals all day over the fire.

Peets had no idea where they had acquired these animals. They looked strange to him and weren't indigenous to Delavia. The sight of the gargantuan Valdons tearing into the flesh of these poor animals made Peets feel sick. The sight, sounds and smells of them tearing into the roasting carcasses was disgusting. The Delavians only ate plants and roots and leaves on Delavia. Eating meat seemed like such a strange and horrible thing to do thought Peets. Oh and of course we eat Honey too he smiled. When we can get it. His thoughts returned to his Father. Where was he?

Suddenly one of the Valdons let out a huge, loud belch. They were guzzling some sort of liquid which was making them increasingly loud and rowdy. They have to go to sleep sometime Peets thought looking at them in disgust. Then I can make my move. All I have to do is wait.

The Feast

Isadora was certain that an hour had passed since Tiamut had left. But unfortunately her watch had stopped working ever since they had entered the underground cavern of the Greys. She had hurried to get ready as she didn't want Tiamut turning back up and her being only half dressed. The door that didn't lock caused her some concern. She had on the beautiful, red silk jumpsuit. And purely by chance, she had quite heavy eye makeup on. She had found a pair of what looked like sunglasses in the dressing table drawer. They had sprayed the makeup on her when she had tried them on. She had been ready for quite a while now and as a consequence of this, had resorted to keeping herself amused by checking out the room. It was like a grotto. It was beautiful, especially with all the candles lit around the room which cast shadows on the uneven cave walls. Isadora walked over to the wall of the cave. She squinted as she noticed the strange markings on there. It was clearly writing in some sort of language that she had never seen before.

Suddenly there was a loud bang on the door. 'Jeez!' Jumped Isadora. 'I guess I didn't need to worry about someone just walking in. Scared me half to death.' She mumbled as she opened her door. 'Tiamut, you scared me half...'
Her words hung in the air.
Time stood still. White noise rushed into her ears.
It wasn't Tiamut at the door.
Standing at the door was the most gorgeous person Isadora had ever seen.

He looked to be about 18 years old, but Isadora reminded herself that the Agarthans seemed to age differently than everyone else given that nobody seemed to be over the age of forty. He had wavy black hair to his chin that was tucked behind his ear on one side. He had the most beautiful face Isadora had ever seen. He was tall, like all the Agarthans were, and wearing really smart ornate clothes in the style of the Agarthans. His black top was like a top and a jacket all rolled into one with the silver spiral insignia on it. The rest of his outfit consisted of tight, cream pants and long black boots which came up to his knees. Isadora went bright red as she realised she was looking at this young man's crotch. Oh god she thought, he is gorgeous.

The young man laughed.

NOOO, Isadora thought. No, not this one. PLEASE tell me this guy cannot hear my thoughts? Isadora pleaded to a force unknown.

'Ah Hi!' Said the gorgeous dark haired young man, obviously just totally hearing what she had been thinking. She thought he had gone a bit red. 'My Father Tiamut apologies but he has been detained on important Agarthan business. He has asked that I escort you to the feast. My name is Adama. And yes although you are right as we do age differently, I am 18.' The young man leaned forward, took Isadora's hand and slowly leant down to kiss it.

Fire burned across Isadora's face. Was she on fire? Had her outfit snagged on one of the candles? Why was she so hot? Adama stood back up and stared intently into her face. 'So you are a surface human?' He said. This was more of a statement than a question. 'Are all surface humans so pretty?' Adama said in awe.

The two stared at each other.

The Scout

The Agarthan scout slipped through the portal and onto Delavia.

It appeared that Valdazar and the Valdon Army had retired to the huge, black spikey ship that was parked in the air above the camp. He had no idea how many were in there. But he had heard that the Valdon Army was huge. He used a piece of advanced Technology to secure the outside of the ship. Trapping whoever was in there inside.

There were about twenty Valdons around a camp fire, who had probably been left to guard Chinga's people. They appeared to be quite drunk. The scout rendered himself invisible by pressing a button on his watch and walked straight up to the drunk Valdons camp. He went round them all and sprinkled something into their huge cups. If they weren't drunk already, they will be soon thought the scout.

He could see the two huge Ancients trapped in a large, makeshift, wooden pen. Well they are not going anywhere he mused.

He could also see a large wooden pen holding the Sasquatch that were Chinga's size. There were larger ones and smaller ones that looked to be children. There was about 3,000 in there. It would be so easy to let them out as the gate was only tied together with vine. But as there was such a large number. It would surely tip Valdazar off. And that would compromise the mission.

'Don't worry,' the scout said under his breath. 'We will free you in the morning. Hang in there my friends.'

He snuck back to the portal and he was gone.

Like a whisper on the wind.

And nobody knew that he had been there.

Adama

Isadora had been the one to speak first. 'Er,....should we get to the feast?' She asked embarrassed.

Adama ran a hand through his hair nervously. 'Yes, definitely, the feast. That's where we are going.' Adama recovered his composure and held out his arm for Isadora to link. 'Shall we go?' He asked.

Isadora stepped out of her room and went to lock it and remembered that there was no lock,

'Ah,' she said making small talk. 'I keep forgetting that there is no lock!'

'What's a lock?' Said Adama quizzically.

'Ah, it's something that stops someone breaking into your room.' Isadora said nervously.

'Why would someone want to break into your room?' Adama said confused.

'Normally to steal your stuff.' Laughed Isadora.

'Why would anyone steal your stuff?' Said Adama.

Isadora looked at Adama and could tell he wasn't joking. She remembered what Tiamut had said about their society not having any money.

'Ah that's right!' said Isadora. 'I forgot that you guys don't have money, so why would you need to steal anything?' She joked nervously.

'What's money?' Asked Adama.

Isadora laughed inside, as they made their way down to the feast.

The Great Escape

Now was the time thought Peets, all of the Valdons had fallen into a drunken stupor.

They were all lying on their backs in various positions, snoring really loudly. He'd experimented by throwing rocks into the camp and they had not stirred. It looked like whatever they had been drinking had knocked them out cold.

Peets took a deep breath and slowly made his way through the camp. He passed the huge sleeping Valdons and over to the pen which held all of the Delavians.

He telepathically communicated with the one nearest the gate where the pen was locked. This one was fast asleep.

'Hey!' Said Peets to the sleeping Sasquatch.

The Sasquatch looked around startled.

'Over here!' Peets said telepathically to the confused furry creature.

The Sasquatch saw Peets and started to stand up, 'Ah thank the creator!' He responded. 'Are you here to save us?'

'Yes, if I can,' said Peets. 'I will concentrate on getting this gate open. You speak to everyone and get them ready to leave. QUIETLY!' Emphasised the small furry creature. 'We don't want these huge things waking up whilst were trying to escape!'

Peets worked on the knotted vine which had been used to tie up the gate on the huge makeshift wooden pen. The Valdons had been so smug thinking that there was no chance that the Delavians would dare escape. That vine from the forest is all that they had used to secure the pen. As he did this he eagerly scanned the Delavians which were slowly but excitedly getting up, for his Mother and Sister. He couldn't see them. His heart started to beat faster and he threw himself into working on the knot. Suddenly he heard his Mothers voice scream 'Peets!' in his head. He looked up and saw his Mother running towards the gate. Peets had never felt such joy in his life. Tears pricked in his eyes and he tried really, really hard to not cry in front of the whole population of his people. 'Mother!' He said telepathically. 'Get everyone in lines and ready to file out. Quietly! I've almost worked this knot free.'

His Sister's voice suddenly popped into his head. 'I knew you would save us Peets!' Said Sneets with a smile. 'I told Mother that you would. Suddenly she looked sad. Have you seen Father?'

'No,' said Peets trying to stifle a sob that was building within his chest. 'I haven't seen him since he left the other night to go Honey fetching.' The brave little Sasquatch said.

'Do you think he's still on the Honey planet?' Said his Sister excitedly. Or maybe he came back but he's just been watching and waiting to rescue us?'

'No,' said Peets. 'If he had come back. He would have tried to save everyone by now just like I'm doing. Plus he'd have connected with us telepathically already. I think he's still on the Honey planet and I don't know why? Somethings wrong. We need to go find him and see if he needs help.'

'How are we?' Began Sneets.

'Shhhhh. Not now we'll discuss it later!' Snapped Peets. For now we need to get our people out before these things wake up.'

Suddenly the knot pulled free in Peets' hands and he quickly pulled back the gate.

He reached out to everyone telepathically.

'Right everyone file out in two's. Quickly but quietly. We want to get everyone out and to safety before these things wake up and try to find us. DO NOT make any noise.'

A Sasquatch that was near the front of the pen suddenly said, 'How come the Valdons can't hear you speaking telepathically now. Like we all can. Aren't YOU going to wake them up?'

Peets looked at the Valdons and then back at his kind.

'I don't think the Valdons know how to speak telepathically. Valdazar had that human slave with him didn't he? That he used to speak to the Ancients? If the Valdons could communicate telepathically. Why would he need the human slave?'

The Sasquatch who had asked this question looked down at his toes.

'Now quickly and quietly everybody,' said Peets. 'Follow me.'

Peets set off walking back round the sleeping Valdons and out of the camp. He kept walking until he had led his people deep into the woods of Delavia. He found an open glade where his people could congregate. He paused to check that everyone had caught up. Slowly and quietly all of his people filed into the glade. It took about 30 minutes until all of his people had joined them in the glade, including the sick male Sasquatch that needed help.

Peets had located his Mother and Sister and was stood with them giving them both a hug.

A very large. Very old Sasquatch began to speak, in a voice filled with gratitude.

'Peets we cannot thank you enough. You have saved all of our people. Even though a lot of our males are sick from the Honey of Earth. We have together managed to help them walk out of there. You are a true hero of our people.' The old Sasquatch motioned to several male Sasquatch who were being propped up by others.

'I'm so happy that I've managed to get everyone out.' Peets said with relief and took a deep breath. 'And now I have to go back.'

'What?!' Hissed his Sister in surprise. 'Peets we've just got out of there, why would you want to go back?'

'I have to go free the Ancients.' Said the little furry creature.

'But they're so fat, they can't walk.' Shouted someone in the crowd. 'How can you help them?'

'Yes,' shouted another. 'And what have they ever done for us? Would they save us if it was the other way round?'

A mutter started to pick up throughout his people.

'I have to try!' shouted Peets. 'Don't you understand? Yes they may have treated us badly through the ages. But they are our people. We are of them. They are of us. We are all of one kind. We are one. My Father always taught me that if someone is in trouble. If there is anything, anything at all that you can do to help. You must always do it. Because to help someone else is to help yourself. I have to go back.'

Peets' Mother was staring at her little Son with tears and love in her eyes.

She had never been more proud of her Son than at that moment.

'I will come with you my Son!' Cried his Mother. Sneets looked at her Mother in shock. She then realised that her Brother and her Mother were right.

'I'm coming with you too.' Sneets smiled looking at her Brother with admiration in her eyes.

'What are *we* going to do?' Shouted someone from the crowd.

'Let's climb to the caves!' Shouted someone else.

Cries of 'Yes, yes let's go to the caves!' rang around the large group of Sasquatch. And they slowly started to file out of the glade in pursuit of the Delavian caves. The caves were in the densest part of the forest and they meandered down quite far into the crust of the planet. If they could make it to the caves and get quite far down in there. The Valdons would have a hard time finding them, particularly because the Valdons were so tall. They would not fit.

Peets nodded his head in agreement. 'Yes go to the caves and go down as far in there as you can. I will let you know when the coast is clear and you can come back out again. Now I need to get going and free the Ancients before those things wake up again.'

Sneets looked at her Brother and shook her head.

'I'm expecting a lifetime of Honey after this Peets!' She teased giving her Brother a hug.

They started their long walk back to the camp with butterflies in their tummies.

The Feast

Isadora was currently sat opposite Adama at the most opulent, incredibly long table.

Isadora looked up and down the table. There must have been five hundred people sat at this long table. Isadora wondered if this was all of the Agarthan people. So their society was no more than about five hundred people in total?

'There's five hundred and twenty six people in total.' Smiled Adama whilst he sipped from a goblet.

'Great!' Thought Isadora. Another hot guy who can read my thoughts.

Both Orion who was seated to her right and Adama laughed at the same time. Isadora rolled her eyes.

The walk down to this huge room where the feast was being held was an incredible one.

They had walked through a *gigantic* sort of underground paradise to get here. There was no other word for it other than paradise. There were fields as far as the eye could see. Beautiful trees and flowers. Isadora could see fields and fields of some sort of crops and vegetables that were being grown. There was a massive underground lake that glistened as if it was made of starlight itself. The birds and butterflies that were flying around were breath taking. This place really was incredible. And it was all under the ground! Isadora couldn't quite believe that she was here. She had to pinch herself. She thought about all that she had done that day. It was really hard to take in. Two days ago she was sat at her desk in school and now she was sat with a different race of humans, about to partake in a feast, under the Earth's crust.

Isadora looked up at Adama. Man he was beautiful, she thought. He had been picking at the fruit on the table whilst intermittently looking at Isadora. He appeared to be fascinated by her. 'So, how did all this come about?' Asked Isadora not really knowing how to kick a conversation off. How did all this come about? Isadora cringed. What a *stupid* thing to say! She squirmed inside and colour streaked up her face.

Adama smiled and looked down at the table and then back up at Isadora. 'Our people moved under the surface of the Earth about 18 million years ago just before a huge cataclysm happened on Earth.'

'Cataclysm?' Isadora said. 'What kind of a cataclysm?'

'It was a comet,' elaborated Adama whilst pouring Isadora some more water. 'We had prior warning of it coming due to our advanced Technology. So we retreated under the Earth and customised some of the larger natural Earth caverns for our purposes. And as you can see, we have everything that we could ever need here. We grow nearly all of what we eat in the Earth here. We have a fantastic society and world. Yet we have the Technology to leave here whenever we want and travel the Universe.' Adama smiled. 'After the comet hit, the surface was uninhabitable for a while. Some of our people decided to stay on the surface and take their chances. And some of them survived as they hid deep down in caves that were on the surface. When the new races of humans arrived on the ships, those of our people who stayed on the surface started breeding with them. And that's where you surface humans come from today.'

'New races of humans?' Exclaimed Isadora in surprise. 'What do you mean?' Suddenly everything that she had learnt in history was starting to seem like a bit of a joke. Was nothing that she had been taught in school correct?

'Yes,' continued Adama clearly enjoying that he was in a position to impress his new female guest. His chest puffed out a bit more. 'A nearby planet in our Solar system had exploded. So after things calmed down, the humans from that planet were rehomed here.'

'I'm sorry,' said Isadora trying to follow what Adama was saying. 'You said re-homed here? What do you mean?' She stared at Adama. His hair was gorgeous. 'Re-homed by who?'

'By various different races of beings actually,' continued Adama. 'Many of them were from the constellation Lyra. Some of them were from the Pleiades.'

Isadora was just about to ask Adama what the hell he was talking about, when the food started to be brought in. It was being brought in by what looked to be the same small grey aliens that she had seen earlier that day at Ebanon's underground base.

'How on Earth did you get these guys to bring in our food?' Isadora laughed astonished. 'Don't they find that a bit beneath them? They were doing experiments the last time I saw them!' Isadora asked puzzled.

'Oh don't worry about that,' said Adama. 'These little guys aren't alive. They're programmable lifeforms. They do what we program them to do. They will be different ones from the ones you will have already seen today. You can pick them up in most places within the Galaxy.' Adama smiled as he started tucking into what had been placed on his plate.

'What the hell?' Thought Isadora as she sat back in her seat. Was anything real? Is anything that I have in my life actual reality? Isadora thought reeling.

'Ah I can answer that question for you Isadora,' interjected Orion pulling Isadora rudely from her thoughts. 'No, nothing that you think is reality, is really reality, it's a crazy world out there Ma-am!' The beautiful Cowboy winked and carried on tucking into the incredible vegetable dish that was sat on their plates with gusto.

Isadora watched all of these beautiful people tucking into their meals and felt like she was sat in a dream. The reality of what had happened to her over the last two days started to sink in and she felt tired. The implications of what this meant for her family and the American people. Hell *all people* also sank in.

There were aliens. Lots of them. There were other planets in the Universe that were habitable. Billions of them. There were a race of early humans who were way more advanced than the current surface humans race were. And they lived underground. They were having this feast under the feet of the people of the surface of the planet and the majority of the human race did not have a clue. Whilst everyone is up there tucking into their microwave dinners and watching Real Housewives of New Jersey, we're under the Earth with Ancient humans and programmable lifeforms and god knows what else! Isadora felt numb. Suddenly her stomach let out a loud rumble.

Orion laughed. 'Eat up Isadora!' He teased wiggling his eye brows. 'You'll need your strength for our trip tomorrow darlin.'

The trip tomorrow Isadora sighed, that was another thing, I don't particularly fancy seeing those creatures again she thought.

He stomach rumbled again. She looked at her plate. The food did look exceptionally good.

'Well there's no point letting good food go to waste.' She said aloud and began tucking in.

It was divine.

The Ancients

Peets, Sneets and their Mother had snuck back into camp. Peets had told Sneets and his Mother to stay on the edge of the camp in case anything went wrong and the Valdons woke up. He would go and try and help the Ancients alone. There was no need for all three of them to get caught if the Valdons woke up. And if the Valdons did wake up, Sneets and their Mother were to run as fast as possible, as far away as possible. Up to the caves.

Peets slowly crept past the still sleeping Valdons, and up to the huge Ancients who were also currently asleep. Peets wondered if the Ancients even knew if the rest of their people had already left the camp.

Peets connected with them telepathically. 'Ancient ones, wake up!' Peets said into their heads.

The Ancients carried on sleeping.

'Please, Ancient ones wake up!' Peets tried again to rouse them from their sleep.

Slowly one of them opened their eyes. Surprise registered on the huge creatures face.

'Ancient ones,' continued Peets. 'How can I help you escape, what can I do?'

The surprise on the huge creatures face slowly turned to sadness.

'There isn't anything that you can do little one. We are doomed.' The monstrous creature spoke directly into Peets' head.

Peets looked frustrated. 'There must be something I can do?' He said. 'If I let you out can you walk? I have helped the rest of our people escape and they are on their way right now to the caves of Delavia to hide. Is there any chance that you could make it there too?'

The Ancient one tried to smile but the folds of fat on his face made even this small movement difficult. 'We cannot walk at all, let alone that far. And even if we could, we are too big to fit down into the caves. There is nothing you can do little one.' The huge creature said. 'This situation is of our own making. We realise this. We have been greedy and foolish over the years. We should have taken better care of our people. We shouldn't have been as greedy and kept all the Honey for ourselves. If we had shared the Honey out we wouldn't be as fat as we are now. And we would be able to walk out of this camp like you are going to do.' The Ancient one looked down and huge fat tears spilled over its eyes. 'But we can't walk out as we are too fat, and that is a situation of our own making and greed. This is karma at its most apparent. It is the law of the creator. What we give out, we ultimately receive and we have given out unkindness and injustice for a very long time. This is now as it should be. Leave my little one and go with our blessing. Free as many of our people as you can.' The huge Ancient said with gratitude and compassion in its voice.

Peets took one more look at the huge Ancient creature and suddenly had an idea. 'I am going to get help for you.' He said trying to reassure the Ancients. 'My Father Chinga has gone to the Honey planet and has not yet come back. If I can find him and ask him to bring help back with him, maybe we can help you escape?' Hope shone in Peets' eyes.

The Ancient one looked at him with love in his eyes. 'What is your name little one?'

'My name is Peets.' Said the little furry creature. 'My Father is Chinga. He has gone to the Honey planet to fetch Honey back for our kind. He went two days ago but he has not come back yet. If I can find him I am sure he will be able to help you.'

'No little one,' said the huge Ancient creature. 'You are very brave but do not follow your Father. Get yourself to the safety of the Delavian caves and wait for your Father to return. We must stay here and await our karma. This is our final decision,' spoke the huge creature. Regret shone in its huge eyes. Peets shook his head, he could not accept this. He could not just let the Ancients still be here when the Valdons woke up. God knows what they would do to them in anger when they realised that the rest had escaped. 'No its ok,' he reassured. 'I will go and fetch help. I'll be back as soon as I can!' He turned on his heels and ran off to join his Mother and Sister as fast as he could.

'NOOOOO Peets!' Shouted the Ancient telepathically in Peets' retreating head. 'Save yourselves we are not worth the risk!'

Peets re-joined his startled Mother and Sister at the edge of the camp.

'I know what I need to do!' He said excitedly and out of breath.

'What Peets?' asked his Mother. 'What did the Ancients say?'

'I need to go and find Father on the Honey planet.' Panted Peets his little chest heaving.

'The Ancients said that?' His Mother questioned angrily. 'Well what a stupid, ill advised..'

'Mother there's no time to explain!' Yelled Peets. 'Come on quick! I know where the place is where Father disappears. I followed him the other night and saw where he went. I can go there and find him and bring help back. I can make it all ok!' The small creature explained happily.

'Peets I really don't think that is a good idea,' shouted Sneets after her departing Brother. But Peets had already set off running for where he had seen his Father disappear. 'What happens if you can't find Father? What happens if Father already came back?' Sneets shouted out of breath as she ran to catch up her Brother.

'If Father had already come back, he would have saved us.' Shouted Peets, running through the trees and towards the portal. 'Besides he would have connected with us telepathically.'

'Peets!' Shouted his Mother. 'Stop! You are not thinking this through!' She screamed. 'Please, I may have already lost your Father, I can't lose you too!' His Mother cried lagging behind.

Peets reached the glade where the portal was shimmering in the distance. All three of them gasped as they could see the bubble shimmering in the dark. Like a giant sparkly dew drop. He turned around with a peaceful expression on his face. 'I need to do this Mother. You have to understand. I have to help the Ancients. I need to find Father. Everything will be ok.' The little one said.

'Peets!' Cried his Mother with tears running down the fur on her face. 'Please, please don't do this! There must be another way!' She stepped towards him as he backed slowly towards the portal.

'Mother is right Peets!' Screamed Sneets. 'Father would be mad with you if he thought that you had followed him to the Honey planet. He would tell you to stay here and look after Mother!' Screamed his Sister desperately.

A look spread over Peets' face. One which his Mother and Sister had not seen before. 'No,' said the little Sasquatch calmly. 'Father would be proud of me that I have tried to help. I have to do this. I love you both. Go back to the caves, I will meet you there with Father when I have found him.' Peets took one more look at his Mother and his Sister and jumped into the bubble. And POP. He was gone.

'Noooooooooooooo!' Screamed Peets' Mother and fell to her knees. 'My boy! My baby boy.'

Her desperate sobs filled the dark of the night.

The Feast

Isadora had started to relax and have a good time. The food was excellent and she was starting to really like Adama. Maybe a little bit too much. He made her tummy feel funny. Like she could almost be sick. But in a good way. He was unlike any other boy she had ever met. He genuinely seemed interested in what her opinion was on things. He laughed at her jokes and he looked like he really found them funny. He seemed totally opposite of any boys she had ever spoken with at school. All of whom seemed to be obsessed with pinging girls bra straps and making farting noises with their hands and arm pits. He wasn't arrogant, he was really knowledgeable and he had spent much of the night filling Isadora in on her own people's history which in itself was mildly embarrassing, but at least they had plenty to talk about. They'd eaten five courses of the most wonderful food. It had all been vegetables and some fish. But it had been cooked in herbs and spices which were nothing that Isadora had ever tasted before. She wondered if the spices had come from somewhere other than Earth. The fact that I'm even thinking that, shows me how far I've come in the last two days she thought to herself with a smile.

Suddenly the table and the room went silent. Kaia stood up. She looked breath taking tonight in a white silk pantsuit similar to the one that Isadora currently had on. Her eyes sparkled in the candle light on the table and her long white blond hair was styled in waves. Adama had told Isadora earlier in the evening that Kaia was 130 years old. Isadora had been astounded when he had told her this as Kaia looked about twenty five. Whatever is in this food Isadora thought, I want to keep eating it if I can look like Kaia when I'm twenty five.

Kaia began to speak into the silence with every pair of eyes in the room on her. 'I would like to formally welcome our new friends Isadora, Chinga, Orion and General Myers to our community here in

Agartha City.' The beautiful woman said. 'And I hope that the work which we are to undertake together tomorrow. Will be conducted as peacefully as possible and will result in the beginning of a very fruitful alliance for all concerned.' The beautiful woman held up her glass and said 'Bless this water with the love and light of the one true creator!' She sipped from the goblet. Everyone else at the table then did the same. 'And now, said Kaia it's time for some dancing.' The beautiful woman smiled and the table disappeared. Isadora realised she was now standing on her feet in the middle of a huge space that was to be used for dancing. Her hands were currently placed in a dancing position with the opposite person to her at the table. Adama. Her heart flip flopped and she could feel her adrenaline spiking. God he smells good she thought. And he looks even better close up. Her revere was interrupted by a shout from General Myers. He had been sat opposite Chinga at the dinner table and they had found themselves in the uncomfortable position of holding hands as dance partners. General Myers stalked off into the crowd leaving a laughing Chinga saying, 'Was it something I said?'

Isadora laughed.

'What is the situation there?' Enquired Adama nodding his head towards Chinga as he began to sway Isadora in rhythm to the music. The music was incredible. It was kind of like Folk, Irish, Scottish and Brazilian all rolled into one. Adama must have read her thoughts. 'We love your music.' He whispered into her ear. She could feel his breath on her skin. It gave her goose bumps. 'Ah, the situation there,' she said flustered, 'is General Myers is a member of our Military and he is pretty up tight. And ah, Chinga my friend is a Sasquatch. And he's from another planet to us.'

Adama nodded his head. 'I wasn't sure whether he was a Sasquatch of Earth as I know some of them still live here. Also there's so many experiments going on on Earth at the moment. You never really know what is from here and what's not.' He laughed and twirled Isadora round.

When Isadora's head had stopped spinning she said, 'Experiments on Earth? What do you mean?'

Adama laughed. 'I keep forgetting that you are not privy to much of what your shadow government does. Experiments with pretty much anything really. They've created hybrids of most things. Combined humans with every animal on your Earth and some animals that are not of your Earth. In order to see what can be created for their use. Mostly for war. It's always about war with surface humans. Where do you think things like the Tuba Cabra comes from? All of their experiments are kept underground in a huge facility built under Sandia Peak in New Mexico. Have you heard of that?'

'Yes,' said Isadora swallowing and feeling sick. 'I've been up there with my Momma and Daddy one vacation on the sky car.' She felt sadness fill her chest when she thought of her Daddy. It had been a lovely day. Bright white sunshine. It had been so exciting in the sky car seeing all of the trees on the mountain on the way up. Daddy was teasing her that the sky car would plummet to the mountain underneath them on the way up. She also remembered a plane that had crashed on there. The debris was still laid out on the floor as it was that high up the mountain no one could get to it. Now Adama was saying there were underground bases under that thing? It seemed a bit farfetched. Part of her felt annoyed about how he was talking about her people. Humans weren't that bad. They wouldn't do that. That would be ludicrous.

Hearing her thoughts Adama smiled and whispered in her ear. 'It may seem like science fiction to you Isadora but it is true. Your people have no idea what is really going on in your own world. Most of it is kept hidden from you.' He lowered his voice, and his stubble tickled her ear. 'If your people knew half of what *really* happens on your planet.' He leaned in closer and his mouth brushed her neck. Her skin prickled and as the hairs on her neck began to zing with electricity. Adama whispered into her ear 'It would make the hairs stand up on your neck.'

Isadora swallowed. Well he was right about that. That was for sure. She frowned. It was not right that the average human had no knowledge of all this. Why was that so? Adama answered this question for her as he twirled her around.

'There are a few in your world who have controlled the many for a very, very long time Isadora. They have done this for their own selfish, greedy reasons to satisfy their need for power.' He pulled back and looked deep into her eyes. 'But I think the time is approaching where this will not be reality for you surface humans for much longer. The *great awakening* is happening.' He whispered in her ear and pulled her closer to him as the music changed into a slow dance.

'The great awakening?' Whispered Isadora. She was feeling a bit intoxicated by the smell of Adama's skin. He was wearing a particular aftershave that she had never smelt before and it made her lightheaded. It was an incredible smell.

'Yes,' said Adama staring into her eyes. Suddenly the ceiling of the huge cavern that they were in changed into the night sky. She let out a gasp. It was breath taking. She had spent much of her life star gazing with her Daddy. Then after he disappeared, watching the stars with her little telescope. She had never seen the night sky look as incredible as this. She suddenly realised why. It was because it was a picture of the sky, from another point in the Universe. Not from our perspective stood on Earth.

Adama read her thoughts. 'Wow!' He smiled pulling back from her and looking shy all of a sudden. 'You are intelligent as well as beautiful. Yes it is the sky that you see when stood on one of the Moons in the Pleiades constellation. We have Technology that has captured the picture of that exact sky. And we can paint it on our ceiling here. It's beautiful isn't it?' He said staring into her eyes. Isadora had never heard of the Pleiades before. But she could agree with Adama that it was beautiful. It was the most beautiful thing that she had ever seen. Adama leaned in closer and the two carried on spinning together under a carpet of stars.

Peets

Peets was not prepared for the sensation he had felt when he had been sucked through the portal. He had been pulled off his feet so fast it had felt like a million threads had been attached to him and had all been pulled at once. As soon as his feet had left the ground they had landed on solid ground again. He leant straight over and vomited on the ground. That was horrible he thought. I had no idea that Father had to do that every time he travelled. Why does he do it? Then his thoughts turned to Honey and how delicious it was. He understood why his Father would put himself through that every time. He stood up straight to survey his surroundings and felt sick once more.

This could not be right.

His Father had explained to him what the Honey planet was like one night as he was tucking Peets in to bed. He said it was very beautiful. But in a different way to Delavia. The colours were different, but the trees and lakes and mountains were the same. He had told Peets that the Honey planet had dense trees much like Delavia. But they were not golden like Delavia. They were green. And the Honey bees lived in these trees. His Father had told him that as soon as he got to the Honey planet. He would sniff the air and he would be able to work out from that which trees had the Honey in. Also his Father had said that he used his acute hearing to locate the buzz of the bees too. Using those two things is how he found them and procured the Honey.

This was not like Peets had expected at all.

He stared around him in disbelief. The planet looked mostly barren. There was rubble and debris everywhere. There a breathable atmosphere but it was very thin and Peets found himself panting as if he couldn't quite get enough air. There were no trees. There were NO trees! He thought panicked. There were no bees!

Panic coursed through his chest and fed his muscles with energy. He spun in a circle in case the trees were behind him. But all around as far as the eye could see was rubble. It was barren.

'No!' Whispered Peets as adrenalin coursed through his body. 'This is wrong. There should be trees! Where's the trees?' Suddenly his bravery left him and his chest started to heave. He couldn't get enough air. He had only wanted to do the right thing and save all of his people and find his Father. He suddenly realised he had made a massive mistake. He should have listened to his Mother, and now he may never see her again. He fell to his knees. 'Father, Father!' He shouted. 'Where are you? Help me! Help me please!'

The furry little Sasquatch sobbed into his hands and the echo's ricocheted into the unknown.

The Best Night

Isadora had had the best night. It had been magical. Adama was incredible and they had danced all night. He had explained so much to her about his culture and also about the history, the true history of her people too. The food, the dancing, the stars. Everything had been perfect. Adama and Isadora were now taking a slow walk up to her sleeping quarters. The room with no lock. Kaia had explained to her earlier in the night that a scout had been sent to Delavia and the mission had been a success. She did not elaborate on that. They were all to meet in the great hall where Isadora's party had originally portalled into, in the morning at 5am sharp. Kaia seemed confident that they would be able to take back Delavia with minimal to no casualties. This made Isadora feel better as the thought of being involved in a war had made her feel very anxious.

As they were walking back to Isadora's room, she suddenly thought about Tiamut. 'Adama!' She said in surprise. 'What happened to your Father? Did he make it to the feast in the end? I didn't see him?'

Adama smiled. 'My Father was the scout that was sent to Delavia.'

Isadora reeled back in shock. 'Oh! Oh my goodness I had no idea. Is he ok? Kaia said the mission went OK but she didn't tell me any more than that?'

'Yes, Father contacted me telepathically when we were dancing earlier. He said it went well. He could only see about twenty Valdons around the camp fire and the rest are assumed to be on the ship. I think that's why we're leaving so early in the morning so we have the element of surprise. We can take the ship whilst most of them are still on there. It should be so quick they won't even realise what's happened.'

'You're coming too?' Asked Isadora shyly. And the significance of that hung in the air. She was desperate to see him again. Isadora suddenly realised that they were in front of her door. Her heart sank. She didn't want the night to end. It had been one of the best of her life.

'I'm glad you've had a good time,' said Adama quietly. 'That makes me happy.' He started to lean in close to her.

Oh my god thought Isadora, he's going to kiss me! *Is he going to kiss me?* She felt sick. No I'm imagining it. Her heart was pounding so hard she thought her chest would explode.

Adama paused and looked in her eyes almost asking for permission.

Please kiss me, Isadora thought as she felt her heart might stop beating.

Adama leant the rest of the way and kissed Isadora. His lips were soft and firm all at once. And warm. Electricity crackled between them. Isadora felt like she was floating on a cloud. Heat rushed into her head and she felt light headed.

It was Isadora's first kiss.

And it was officially *the* best night of her life.

Valdar

Valdazar was starting to get bored again. Like with anything new, it held his attention for a short while and then the itching in his soul came back. The boredom. The need to torture somebody or conquer a planet. The need to prove himself. The need to be feared and revered. His new toy had pleased him for a time. But now he needed a new focus.

'When was the last time we returned to Valdar Human?' Valdazar asked his slave.

'It has been some time Sire since we were last on Valdar.' Said Human quietly.

'Yes, yes it has. I feel the need to re-acquaint myself with home don't you Human?' Giggled his master with glee.

'Yes, more than you know.' Thought Human sadly.

Valdazar placed his hands on the driving plate of the spaceship and thought about Valdar. Suddenly a swirling image of his planet popped up on the screen at the front of the ship.

The planet looked much like Valdazar's original ship. It was a dark planet. Very scary looking. Where much of the surface was covered in large Stalagmites. That's where he had got the idea from for his original ship which was covered in spikes. He had loved that ship when it had first been made.

'Right then Human. Let's go back to Valdar and I think we will have a feast tonight in my honour. For being an unbeatable, almighty conqueror!' Valdazar laughed an evil laugh. 'And we can plan tonight where we will hit next.'

'Yes Sire.' Said Human quietly as his thoughts turned to his home. Earth. I wonder how my family are? I wonder if they are still looking for me? Or if they think I am dead? Probably better that they think I am dead he thought sadly. As I will never get to see them again. There is no escape from this mad man.

Human closed his eyes and replayed a scene in his mind of when his daughter was young and they were building a snowman outside.

Suddenly he realised that they were at Valdar as the ship had stopped. This ship was very fast, much faster than his master's last one. The speed with which they had travelled shocked Human. This ship was very powerful indeed.

'Human!' Barked Valdazar. Let the kitchen know that I am back and I expect the best food that they have ever produced tonight in my honour and for my entire army. I want a feast of epic proportions.'

'Yes master,' said Human sadly. He stepped out off the ship and into the darkness.

Simud

Peets could not believe how stupid he had been. Why did he just jump into the portal? He should have waited for Father to come back like Mother had said. He remembered now his Father telling him that he only went Honey fetching when the portal was open. He hadn't really known what he had meant at the time. But whilst he was sat here in the dirt with his head in his hands. He realised what his Father had meant. His Father only went through the portal at set times when the portal came to the Honey planet. The rest of the time, it didn't go there. It went somewhere else. That's why his Father had not come back yet. He must have for some reason missed the opening for coming back through the portal on the night he left, and he had been waiting for it to re-open again so he could return. Why couldn't he have waited? Now he may never see his Father or his Mother and Sister again.

He let out another loud sob of anguish.

'Shhhhhh!' Hissed a voice from behind him. 'Get in here before they find you!'

Peets jumped a foot and turned round to see where the voice was coming from.

He squinted and peered into the distance. He could not see anything. Where was the voice coming from?

'Quick!' Said the voice again. 'You've made enough noise to alert them all. Get in here quick and hopefully you'll stand a chance of surviving.'

Suddenly within the rubble on the floor, Peets saw the mouth of a cave. His eyes focussed on it.

'Yes that's right,' said the voice. 'Come into the cave, now!'

Peets wiped his nose and took a deep breath. Over the distance along the large expanse of rubble he could see stretching out in front of him, he could hear a noise coming closer to where he was. Dust was flying into the air.

'Come now! Because once they get over that ridge, there will be no escape!' Shouted the voice. 'COME NOW!'

Peets had to make a decision. The voice sounded friendly like it was trying to help him. And he could use a friend right now.

He ran towards the voice and jumped into the cave. Just before a car careered over the ridge and screeched to a stop.

The Mission

Isadora was woken the next morning at 4.30am by the voice of Kaia telepathically in her head.

'Isadora it's time to get up,' Kaia said softly. 'You have thirty minutes till we meet in the great hall.

'OK thanks,' said Isadora to the voice in her head in surprise. She was still getting used to this. It was so strange to have so many people be able to hear her thoughts. She was going to have to work on keeping her inner voice to a minimum she sighed. She had no idea if Kaia could hear her back. She waited to see if Kaia said anything else as she rubbed sleep from her eyes. She must have gone.

Isadora's cheeks went red and a huge smile spread over her face when she remembered the events of the previous night. She had kissed a boy. For the first time. Well he had kissed her. And she had let him. And it had been fantastic. Embarrassment coursed through her veins. What if he regretted it this morning? She had to see him again today as he was coming on the Delavia mission. What if they didn't have anything to say to each other?

She shoved a pillow over her face and cringed. He must have thought she was so stupid as she didn't know *anything* about the history of her own people. Let alone his. But he had said that he thought she was intelligent. So maybe not. It wasn't her fault that surface humans were kept in the dark about pretty much everything that was happening on their planet. She did feel stupid. How could it be that we don't know about any of this stuff? Adama had said that a few people on our Earth had controlled the masses for years. Who did he mean? She'd heard about all the rumours of secret societies and the Illuminati and Cabal etc. She'd watched the Di Vinci code and Angels and Demons. But that was all legend and folklore right? It wasn't real? If it was real it wouldn't be in the movies? If it was real, people would be up in arms right now asking the Cabal why the hell they controlled our planet and who did they think they were making all the decisions for us, right?

She scratched her head. Isadora would love to think more about this. But she had to get up, get ready and meet everyone in the great hall.

She was just thinking what should I wear? When she saw the clothes folded up on the bottom of her bed. Hmmmmmm she frowned. The unlocked door. She quickly got dressed and ran a comb through her hair and ran down to the hall where they had portalled into the night before. She felt embarrassed when she realised she was the last to arrive from her own party. Orion, Chinga and General Myers were already there. Stood with Kaia, Tiamut, Hyperion, a woman that Isadora had not seen before and Adama. She shyly looked up at Adama and he returned her glance with a warm smile. Instantly she feel better.

'Morning,' Adama said smiling shyly. 'Did you sleep well?'

'Yes,' said Isadora trying not to go red when she started thinking about kissing him again. 'I never even heard whoever it was that brought my clothes in in the night!' She laughed nervously.

'Ah yes,' said Adama teasing. 'The unlocked door. Did anyone steal your stuff?' He smiled his eyes dancing.

'Ah, no, no one stole my stuff.' She laughed awkwardly.

Their conversation was interrupted by one more male joining their party. He looked to be in soldier attire albeit in the ornate style of the Agarthans. He nodded at Kaia.

'OK,' Kaia began. 'Our party is now complete. We are the ten who will be taking back Delavia.'

Ten? Isadora thought panicked. That is not enough? There were a hundred of those huge creatures on Delavia. How were we supposed to defeat them with ten people?

'Do not worry Isadora!' Kaia said as she could obviously hear her panicked thoughts. 'We will be stopping off somewhere on the way to pick up re-enforcements. But I am very confident that we will not need them. Our plan is to get to Delavia and deal with the Valdons on the ground first. Tiamut has said there are twenty. He slipped them a drug which should keep them sleeping for at least two days so we should be able to control them no problem.'

'The rest are on the ship. We have the Technology to 'take' the ship peacefully. They will have no choice but to surrender. Tiamut also put a lock on the ship so they can't get out until we release them. Hopefully the mission should not take long at all.'

'Where are we stopping off for reinforcements?' Asked Isadora, wondering how this was all going to work. How were they even going to get to Delavia?

'We will be going to the Moon for reinforcements Isadora' smiled Kaia.

Isadora swallowed. The Moon?

The Bears

Peets blinked furiously as his eyes adjusted to the darkness.

'You made the right choice my friend,' said the voice. 'If you have stayed in plain sight for a moment longer, you would have been captured.'

'Captured by who?' Asked Peets. His eyes were still not working properly in the darkness. He could see the outline of a large shape but that was it.

'By the humans!' Said the gruff, deep voice shuddering.

'Humans?' Exclaimed Peets in surprise and a bubble of hope popped up in his chest. 'Then I am on Earth? I made it to the Honey planet?' His Father had always spoken about the humans and how they lived on the Honey planet. But that you must always, always avoid being seen by the humans at all costs. They did not like sharing their planet with each other, let alone people from other planets. It was well known that if you were seen on Earth by a human they would shoot you first and ask questions later.

'Oh no my friend,' chuckled the voice. The shape of which was starting to become clearer. 'You are definitely not on the Honey planet. For I don't know what Honey is and my kind have been here since the beginning of time.'

Peets' heart sank as he listened to the voice but slowly his vision started to come back to him. He smiled as he stared straight into the face of a huge sandy coloured bear. Its shaggy fur was the same colour as the rocks of the landscape. It was huge. As big as a full grown Sasquatch. But it walked on all fours, not two like the Sasquatch did.

'Hi!' Smiled the furry little one. 'I'm Peets. I'm looking for my Father. He came to the Honey planet to fetch Honey for my people and he hasn't been back since. I followed him into the portal and it brought me here. But this isn't the Honey planet you say?' Peets was confused.

'No, my friend it is not,' said the huge bear gravely. 'This planet has had many names throughout the ages. It has been known as Simud by some in ages past. Others have called it Auqakuh or Harmakhis. But I believe the name that it is most commonly known as in the age that we are in now, is Mars.'

Mars thought Peets. Where is Mars?

The Sea of Ships

'The Moon!' Exclaimed Isadora in disbelief. 'As in the Moon that's in our sky? As in the one that's supposed to be made of cheese? What? Why do we need to go to the Moon? How are we even going to get to the Moon?' She asked Adama as they were walking quickly to a destination unknown. Isadora could not get her head around this new development at all. This of all the things that had happened to her over the last couple of days was too much. She was beginning to think that she really was losing her mind.

Adama smiled at Isadora. 'Don't worry Isadora. We will be going to the Moon in one of our ships. Our Silver Fleet. We do it all the time. It is nothing to be worried about. It's just as simple as you guys getting in your car and going to the shops for milk. We have very advanced Technology which allows us to travel anywhere we wish in the Universe in seconds. It is very quick.'

Isadora doubted very much that it was like going for milk. 'Advanced Technology? What kind of advanced Technology?' Said Isadora panting. She was almost running to keep up, as the Agarthans were leading them down a series of corridors to somewhere.

'Superluminal travel,' said Adama as if it was the most natural thing in the world.

'Superler – what?' Exclaimed Isadora actually breaking onto a jog to keep up.

They had reached an elevator that was imbedded in the rock. Kaia summoned the elevator presumably with her mind, as there were no buttons. They stepped in.

As soon as they stepped in, they were stepping out of the elevator. Isadora's chin hit the floor. In front of her as far as the eye could see, were a fleet of *huge* spaceships. I mean they were massive. Some were bigger than others. Some were smaller. There was one really huge one which looked like it was miles wide. The hanger that these craft were in stretched as far as the eye could see. Isadora could not see the end.

'Which one are we going in?' Breathed Isadora in amazement.

Kaia turned round to face the party. 'We will be going in two ships. Isadora, Chinga, Orion, Tiamut and I will be going in one ship. Hyperion, Rala, Centaurus, Adama and General Myers will be going in the second ship.'

Isadora felt a bit crest fallen at this. She was hoping that she was going to be able to travel with Adama. They both looked at each other and smiled. An awareness hung in the air between them that something special had happened last night and they weren't quite sure what it was. Tiamut saw this exchange between his Son and the surface human and quickly looked at Isadora with a look of what appeared to be fury on his face.

Isadora looked down and her face flushed. Why would Tiamut be mad with her? Had she done something wrong? Adama did not look mad with her? She looked back up at Tiamut and his face was the same as it had been before. Happy and warm. Maybe she had imagined it? What with everything that had been going on recently, she was likely just frazzled.

Isadora wondered why Kaia had chosen the combination of people that she had chosen to go in the two ships. And then she realised that all the group, including Adama that were in the same ship as General Myers, looked more like Military. Her group looked more like the entertainment. Especially given that Orion had somehow procured a brand new Cowboy outfit in the middle of Inner Earth that was emerald green and sapphire blue.

'How in the hell?' Thought Isadora. Where did he get that from?

Orion turned and winked at her. 'It's beautiful isn't it? Kaia knew someone who could help me out. What?' He fained surprise. 'I'm Orion! I have to have my Cowboy outfit on!' He laughed. Kaia smiled.

'OK,' said Kaia. 'Is everyone clear on the mission and what we are doing?'

No-one spoke.

'Just to reiterate, we will be going to Delavia via the Moon to pick up General Myers' reinforcements. Then we will be journeying to Delavia and hopefully arriving early enough to use the element of surprise to our advantage and take back Delavia in the process. We will be doing this peacefully. The Valdons that are not on the ship are drugged. The Valdons and Valdazar that are inside the ship are locked in on there.'

'Hyperion,' said Kaia. 'Your ship will concentrate on rounding up the Valdons who have been drugged and containing them until our ship has taken control of Valdazars ship. Once we have taken control of Valdazars ship. You can bring the drugged Valdons on. Then we can escort Valdazar out of Delavia and fly with him till he goes home. One of our ships will stay behind on Delavia until we are sure that Valdazar is not coming back. Hyperion, Tiamut, Rala, Centaurus, Adama, you will stay on Delavia and keep it secure until we are satisfied that the Delavians can once again be left to their own devices.'

'I will then fly Isadora, Orion and General Myers back home. Assuming that Chinga will be wishing to stay on his home planet of Delavia reunited with his family.'

Kaia smiled at Chinga. Chinga smiled back. 'Thank you so much for helping us Kaia,' said Chinga. 'Thanks to all of you!' Chinga directed at the rest of the Agarthans party. The rest of the Agarthans smiled back and nodded.

'OK then if everyone is ready, shall we do this?' Said Kaia.
Everyone nodded.

'Right!' said Kaia. 'I will punch out first. Hyperion you follow my lead.'

Hyperion nodded.

Suddenly the floor that they were stood on started to move downwards and join with the floor that the ships were parked on.

Kaia walked up to the first huge ship. 'OK, Hyperion. We will meet you at the Moon,' reconfirmed Kaia. And she opened the door on the ship.

The huge door opened up and Kaia, Isadora, Orion, Chinga and Tiamut filed onto the ship. It was huge inside and very minimalist. It wasn't like star wars. Where you would see a ship and it had a million blinking lights on the inside. There wasn't much at all really. In fact Isadora had no idea how Kaia was going to fly this thing. There didn't seem to be any buttons at all? Kaia sat at the front of the ship with Orion and put her hands on the ships plate. It started up seemingly with her thoughts.

The ship slowly raised up into the air of the cavern, straight up. Isadora's stomach went a bit funny. I wonder what Adama is doing now she thought.

Orion suddenly looked back at her and frowned.

What's his problem she thought? I've never seen him frown before? Just as a blinding light flashed and suddenly they were out in the early morning dusk of the outside world. Fog hung in the air. How the hell did that happen? Thought Isadora in shock. One minute they were in the huge underground Hangar and the next they were outside on the surface. The huge ship purred slowly through the air and Isadora realised that the shimmering, sparkly thing that they were currently approaching was the surface of the sea. Where were they? She thought. That was definitely the sea. What's going to happen now? It looked like the ship was going to go into the sea. Surely that wasn't going to happen? This thing would leak right? It would blow up?

Isadora screamed as the ship plunged forcefully into the ocean. It started to submerge itself and sink deeper and deeper into the darkness below.

Orion who was sat in front of Isadora in the ship now turned round and smiled at her. 'Scream if you wanna go faster!' He winked. But his eyes weren't dancing like normal.

'What are we doing Orion?' Said Isadora in panic as the ship sank further into the ocean. 'I thought we were supposed to be going to the Moon?'

'This is the fastest way to the Moon Isadora,' smiled Orion. 'Relax, Kaia knows what she's doing.'

Suddenly in the darkness of the foreboding depths of the ocean, Isadora saw what looked like a whirlpool in front of the ship. She squinted to get a better look at the vast expanse of water deep in the ocean that was swirling around at a rapid rate.

'What is that?' screamed Isadora hiding her face in her hands.

'It's a Vortex Isadora,' said Orion as if Isadora understood what he was talking about. 'We'll soon be at the Moon don't worry!' Orion teased.

The ship glided closer to the furious whirlpool, the noise was deafening. Isadora closed her eyes and prayed. She prayed to get out of this alive. She had never been as scared in her life. The noise was deafening as the ship entered the Vortex. There was a loud slurp and popping sound. A huge pulling feel. And then POP. The slurping sound stopped. There was only silence. Isadora opened her eyes and nearly fainted. The ship was hovering about a hundred meters above the surface of the Moon.

And in the distance, winking and shimmering. Like a beautiful, iridescent blue and yellow pearl, was Earth.

Mars

Peets stared at the Bear. 'Mars?' Repeated the little Sasquatch. 'Where is Mars?'

The bear smiled at Peets. 'I know not where Mars IS little one. I only know that Mars is here. And we are on it.'

Peets sat down on the floor of the cavern and rubbed his face. What did he do now? What *could* he do now? He had tried to help the Ancients by going through the portal to the Honey planet to find his Father. And in doing so he had ended up *here*. And now his Mother and his Sister had been left on their own on Delavia. What would happen when the Valdons woke up? Would they hunt their people down? Would they find the caves? Would Mother and Sneets make it to the caves before the Valdons woke up? Peets felt sick. No he thought. Mother and Sneets would be waiting around the portal for him to come back with his Father. Only he wouldn't be coming back with his Father. Because he was on Mars, not the Honey planet. Peets put his head in his hands and sobs started to shake his chest once more. What happened when the Valdons woke up and they realised that his people had gone? They would contact Valdazar and he would come back and hunt their people down again. Only this time he would be really mad. He would not be there to protect his Mother and Sister and neither would his Father. What had he done? He had let his whole family down. He had let his people down. He had tried to protect them. He had tried to help and in doing so, he had made things worse. Why did he always think that he could help? Why didn't he listen!

'What is wrong my friend?' Said the huge shaggy bear as he came across the cave to comfort the little Sasquatch.

'I've ruined everything!' Sobbed Peets. 'Everything! I tried to make things better but I have only made things worse. I went through the portal to find Father. To see if he could help me save the

Ancients. And I thought I was going to the Honey planet. But instead, it has brought me here. To this place. There are no trees. There are no bees. There are no humans to help us on Delavia.' Peets chest heaved as his heart broke. He could barely get his breath.

'I do not know of trees or bees my friend and what these things are that you speak of. But there are certainly humans here. But I do not think that these humans can be the people of whom you speak. As these humans will not be able to help anyone.' Said the large bear in a quizzical tone.

Peets tried to stop crying and looked at the bear. 'Why wouldn't they be able to help me?' He sniffed.

'They would not be able to help you my friend. As they are enslaved themselves.' Said the huge bear sadly.

'Who has captured them?' Exclaimed Peets. Wondering if Valdazar had somehow managed to conquer this place too.

'It appears that they are kept captive by their own people.' Said the huge bear. 'The Humans are a war mongering, aggressive and unstable race. We remember when they first arrived here. It was about one hundred years ago now. Prior to the humans, we had been living peacefully on Mars for eons. At least ever since the last Great War in any case. There were many species on this planet that had learnt to live alongside each other peacefully. One day the humans came.' The great bear shuddered and sounded sad. He stared off far into the distance, reliving the scene in his memory.

'They landed in huge black ships and began trying to take over all of the highly sort after refuge places on this planet. They tried to take over the lava tubes and began chasing out the indigenous species that lived in there. However, the humans underestimated the power of the insectoids that live in the lava tubes. They would not give these up without a fight and they were willing to die for their possession of them. The humans were chased away by the great numbers of insectoids that lived in the lava tubes. There are millions upon millions of insectoids living in those lava tubes. Great big creatures at least 8 feet tall with hard insectoid shells for skin. The humans did not expect that and they retreated. They flew away in their big black ships. That night we celebrated. We thought that they had left for good.' The great bear paused and looked directly at Peets. 'We were wrong.'

'The humans returned many years later. But this time they returned with weapons. Frightening weapons which they dropped on our planet and they blew away great holes. They killed a lot of our kind to gain their foothold here. They killed a lot of all kinds in order to build their colonies under the surface of the planet. Millions of the insectoid race died when they dropped their weapons. When the humans had cleared away the space underground that they wanted to use. About 35 years ago they brought more of their kind with them. At first we were scared as we thought that with their increased numbers they would try to kill all of our kind that were left. But we were surprised when it appeared that the additional people that they had brought with them, were their slaves too. Yet they were of their own kind? We could not understand it at first. We tried to make sense of it and watched the humans as closely as we would dare get without being captured.' The bear paused as he gathered his thoughts.

'We were surprised to see over time. That the humans that are held captive, appear to be making things for the humans in charge. Technology. Ships. Other species come here and pick the ships up and take them away. The humans who are held captive appear sad, gaunt and unhappy. The humans that are in charge are evil and nasty and control the masses through fear. But also, assumingly from the knowledge that the incarcerated humans cannot escape. They are held captive here.'

'These humans in charge are unbelievably evil and have no care or compassion for their kind that they are keeping trapped on this planet. They work them to the bone. The one in charge they call

Eldon. He is the most evil being we have ever experienced. He tortures the humans. We have even seen him murder some of them.'

Peets shuddered. 'These humans sound terrible. My Father said that there are humans on the Honey planet or Earth as it is called, and that you must stay hidden from them. But I always just thought that they would be nice? Well they must be as otherwise there's no way that Father would go there all the time?'

The huge bear gasped and turned to look at the small creature. 'Oh my poor little one. Is your Father on the Honey planet? The one that is called Earth?'

Peets noticed the fear in the Bears eyes and started to feel fear in his own chest.

'Yes, Father is on the Honey planet, whose name is Earth. Why?' Peets said shaking. Not wanting to know what he had already begun to think.

The huge bear had tears swimming in his large eyes. 'My child, Earth is where *these* humans are from. If your Father is there, then I am afraid that it may be too late for you to save him. If they can do this to their own kind. What do you think they will do to your Father?'

Peets' legs gave way and he sat down on the cold surface of the cave.

What did he do now?

The Moon

Isadora could not *believe* this was happening. She just could not believe it. From as far back as she could remember, she had always been in love with the Moon. Her Daddy would take her out star gazing when she was a child and she would sit with her Daddy for hours looking at the Moon through her little telescope. Her Daddy would have loved this she thought and her heart broke. He always used to tease her that it was made out of cheese. She laughed and closed her eyes at the power of that memory. Hot tears spilled over her eyes and onto her cheeks. He would not believe where I am now she thought and her heart both broke and soared at the same time. Never in my life did I ever dream it would be possible to come here she thought to herself. '*Daddy I'm on the Moon,*' she whispered as the emotion threatened to burst open her chest.

The Vortex that they had disappeared into in the ocean appeared to somehow be connected to the Moons atmosphere. They had popped right out a few hundred feet above the surface of the Moon. Isadora questioned how on Earth this could happen? Well I suppose it stops the average person on the planet noticing every spaceship flying through the sky on route to the Moon, she laughed to herself. But in all seriousness, how many of those Vortex things were there? And how many ships were flying to the Moon on a daily basis? It was just unbelievable. It's like an unseen world happening and no one on Earth has any idea that this is possible.

As they hovered above the surface of the Moon and made their decent to land, it occurred to Isadora that there couldn't be that many people flying to the Moon as most average humans on Earth didn't even know that this was possible. But the fact that it could be done so covertly without anyone realising it, seemed really sneaky. It also occurred to her that all these rockets that Nasa were making a big deal about sending up to the Moon. Were just a cover for what was really going on. According to Adama, the elite surface humans as well as the Agarthans had Technology which could take you to the Moon as quickly as they had just done. He had told her that last night as they had been twirling under the projected canopy of stars. Well he'd told her about the advanced flying Technology that surface humans had but kept secret. Not necessarily that they went to the Moon with it. She thought about Adama again and her stomach did a flip flop.

Isadora jumped as Kaia started speaking telepathically in Isadora's head. 'We are going to land on the Moon in a moment Isadora as there's also something that I need to collect whilst we are here.'

'Ah OK', thought Isadora. So I'm actually going to get to walk on the Moon she thought. That is amazing.

Kaia spoke inside Isadora's head again, 'Yes the Moon is pretty incredible the first time you ever see it, from this angle at least. The Moon is a very, very important place Isadora. It is the only place within this Galaxy which is a neutral zone.'

'Neutral zone?' Questioned Isadora. 'What do you mean?'

'For many, many years now. Our people have been at war with different races of beings that frequent planet Earth. There have been many wars fought over Gaia and over the Moon. A lot of blood has been shed over the possession of the Moon itself. It is highly sought after as it is in a perfect location to use as a base to be able to visit Gaia whenever you want. Many races of aliens have possessed the Moon over the years and lost it. Until the Great War. During the Great War most of the alien races who were fighting over the Moon nearly wiped themselves out over the possession of this artificial satellite. During those dark times a treaty was drawn up and signed by all involved that no more blood would ever again be shed on the Moon and it would be a neutral zone for all races, and all could land here. Kaia paused.

'Kind of like a big Switzerland?' Isadora exclaimed.

Kaia smiled and Isadora could hear it in her voice. 'Yes Isadora that is correct. Like a big Switzerland. It could also be likened to the Antarctic as many of your countries have pieces of land there which they believe to be their own and it is also another neutral zone. Here on the Moon there are races of aliens who have been at war with each other for thousands of years in various parts of the Galaxy. Yet they have bases on the Moon right next to each other.'

Isadora felt sick. 'Does Valdazar have a base on the Moon too?' She asked as a cold chill ran up her spine.

'No Isadora. He does not as he is not of this Galaxy. He did not fight in these wars where all races have spilt blood. The wars I speak of are Ancient wars. Valdazar is very, very young in celestial terms. But if he keeps conquering planets within this Galaxy then he may well decide that he deserves his piece of the Moon. Or even worse decide that the Moon itself belongs to him. Then the great wars will start all over again. No-one wants to go back to that. Which is one of the reasons that we have agreed to help you. We will be landing at Lunar Operation Command (LOC). This base is used by both surface humans and the Agarthans too when we have need. Which is not very often.' Kaia finished as she slowly landed the huge spacecraft onto the surface of the Moon.

As they had been talking. Isadora had noticed a small building on the surface of the Moon which looked to be built into the side of a crater. It was surrounded by an expanse of broken up rocks. Kaia slowly landed the huge Agarthan ship as near as she could get to the building without landing on the uneven rocks. It looked like they would have to walk some of the way. Isadora could see that Hyperion was also doing the same with the second ship and had begun to land as near to Kaia's ship as possible.

Kaia turned around to look at the inhabitants of the ship with a smile on her face. 'Right then, we had best put on the necessary gear.' Kaia looked at Orion and all of a sudden his beautiful new Cowboy outfit had been replaced by what looked to be some sort of spacesuit. He looked crest fallen. Kaia smiled like she had been waiting to do this. Isadora looked at Kaia in alarm.

'Do not be alarmed Isadora,' smiled Kaia. As Kaia said this she looked at Isadora and a spacesuit appeared on Isadora's body. 'These suits are necessary due to the atmosphere. The Moon does not have one and you need to be able to breathe when we get out there.'

Isadora looked down at herself and smiled. She was wearing a spacesuit. This was so cool. The ones she had seen on TV had always looked so bulky. But this one wasn't. It was mostly white with bits of silver on it and it wasn't heavy to walk in at all. She looked up just as Chinga was being given his spacesuit and laughed out loud at the look on his face. Chinga was not used to wearing clothes.

When all the spacesuits had been given out by Kaia, she somehow imagined one on herself too. How did she do that thought Isadora? It was like magic. But she knew that it wasn't magic. It was something different than that. It was like she did it with her thoughts. But how could you change things just by your thoughts? Isadora tried to change her spacesuit into the colour red which was her favourite colour, just by using her thoughts. Nothing changed. It was still white. She frowned. How does Kaia change things with her mind? How does she fly a ship with her mind? Adama said that the Agarthans were Human just like us. Yet they can do so much more than us? How can that be?

'That's a conversation for another time Isadora,' interrupted Kaia smiling, obviously hearing Isadora's thoughts. 'But whilst we're on the subject Isadora. You need to learn how to guard your thoughts, so they are still your own. At the moment, anyone who is telepathic can listen in. And this leaves you vulnerable. I'm sure there's certain things that you wish would rather remain private?' Kaia teased by showing her a picture of Adama in her mind. Isadora blushed. Yes, it would be excellent if Adama could not read my thoughts she cringed. 'It's really simple Isadora but you will need to practice. Just imagine a shield of white light around your mind. Imagine it guarding your thoughts. You can put it there whenever you want. Practice and it will get easier and easier. Then no one will be able to listen into your thoughts unless you allow them to. The more you practice imagining this shield of white light, eventually, no one will be able to scan your mind without you consciously letting them in.'

Ah ok? Thought Isadora. How on Earth did that work?

'Do not worry about it now Isadora,' finished Kaia. 'But it's something to practice for later. Now, we need to go and pick up what I need to pick up whilst General Myers collects his reinforcements. Follow me!' Said Kaia and the ships huge door opened.

What does Kaia need to pick up thought Isadora and who are General Myers reinforcements?

Valdar

Valdazar sat at the head of a huge table. It was in the main hall of his very big, very dark, very scary castle. Down the length of the table sat all of his Valdon Army. Apart from the ones that he had left at Delavia of course. They were all currently tucking into the feast that he had ordered. It was good to be back home Valdazar mused as he stretched out his long legs. He had missed his cook's food. He stared at all of his vile beasts slurping and ripping into their food and he smiled. He loved being the leader of the Valdons. They were disgusting brutes. Huge, ugly and barbarous. But stupid. That was the best part he giggled as he picked meat from his teeth. They were completely stupid and he could make them do whatever he wanted. He could make them do whatever he wanted *as they feared him.* They feared him as he was ruthless. He had shown them that time and time again. There was nothing that he would not do in order to acquire what he wanted and they revered this about him. He gave them what they needed. Someone to fear and love and worship and follow all rolled into one. They needed direction and he gave them that in abundance.

When Valdazar had initially arrived on Valdar, he was dazed and confused. He didn't know what had happened. One minute he was on Earth. The next he was on Valdar, surrounded by the Valdons who were in the middle of some Ancient ritual. He had been 11 years old at the time. He had been on Earth in bright baking hot sunshine one minute. The next he had appeared on the top of a huge stone in the middle of the night, under a carpet of stars. To the loud chanting of the Valdons screaming 'Valdazar, VALDAZAR!'

At first Valdazar had been scared. He was ashamed to say, he had wanted to cry out for his Mother. As his eyes adjusted to the darkness of the night from the brightness of the sun, he saw what was making the chanting noises and was horrified. He definitely wanted his Mother then. Who were these huge giants and what did they want with him? Where was he? But he very quickly sensed that these huge disgusting beasts thought he was a God. They were bowing to him. They were excited to see him. They were *convinced* he was a God. As he had suddenly just appeared before them right in the middle of some Ancient ritual that was to do with a prophesy. He had just popped up there. On that huge stone which was placed on the top of the tallest hill on Valdar. Right when they were chanting for his appearance. He began to smile as he recalled the events. The night that he *became* Valdazar. The Valdons were chanting for his appearance as there was an Ancient prophesy on Valdar. The prophesy said that when the time was right, a Demon would appear to the Valdons. This Demon would lead them to their ultimate victory over the whole of the Universe. When he had appeared on Valdar in the middle of their stupid ritual, they had thought he was *that* Demon. He knew he wasn't. He was just some kid, who had somehow been summoned to another world. But the idea had occurred to him to play along as he absolutely loved having these monstrous, strong beasts undertake his every whim and cower before him. It had appealed to him the idea of being a god as he had always known he was special. He loved ordering these stupid creatures around. He enjoyed getting these brutes to torture and kill whoever he wanted. Whenever he wanted. Over time, he had begun to think that the prophesy was right. He had been summoned for a reason. That he *was* a Demon. That he was *the* Demon. That he was a *god. That he actually was Valdazar.* He was Valdazar and he was in charge of a huge army of vile, murderous, stupid, controllable creatures.

Valdazar smiled and ripped into another rib of meat.

And he was going to take over the *Universe*. Oh yes.

Koro

Peets stared into space. All of what the bear had just told him filtered down into his conscious. He had to somehow get back to Delavia. Or if not Delavia. He had to somehow get to Earth and find his Father. If Father could get back to Delavia now whilst there were only a handful of Valdons there, then they could overthrow them and stand a chance of taking their planet back. He had to somehow try and get back. He jumped up and went to thank the bear for his help.

'Thank you so much for saving me,' said Peets. 'I don't even know your name?'

The huge shaggy bear smiled. 'I am Koro, said the bear. And I am a friend to you here.'

'Thank you,' said Peets gratefully. 'But I have to go now Koro. I have to find my Father or at least get back to Delavia and help Mother and Sneets get back to safety.' Peets turned to start walking out of the mouth of the cave.

'What are you doing?' hissed Koro loudly and the echoes travelled all around the cave bouncing off the walls. The noise was deafening. Reverberating over and over. 'Has nothing of what I have just said to you sunk in?' Hissed the bear.

'I have to go back to the portal. I have to go home,' cried Peets. 'I have to find Father. I have to try!'

'If you go back out there to that portal, they will capture you. The humans will capture you. You must stay here.' Koro said gravely. 'If you do not believe me, go back and see for yourself. Get caught and all will be lost. You will never escape them. For even their own kind cannot escape them. Eldon sees all and knows all.' The great bear shook his head as he could see the determination in the little Sasquatch's eyes.

'I have to try, thank you for being kind to me Koro.' Said Peets with sadness in his heart to be leaving his new friend. He stepped out of the cave and began to slowly crawl back over the sand and up to the brow of the small hill that partially covered the entrance of the cave. As Peets got to the top he carefully peeked over the brow of the hill and down to where the portal was. His heart sunk. Koro was right. There were two humans stood directly in front and behind the shimmering bubble of the portal that Peets had come through. They were guarding the portal now. Both humans were holding guns. There was no way through the portal without getting shot by the humans. Peets laid with his back on the sand and tears leaked out of his eyes again. What did he do now?

The low, gravelly, kind voice of Koro whispered from the mouth of the cave.

'There is another portal on this planet my friend and I know where it is.'

Peets slowly made his way back down to where Koro stood and back into the cave.

'What did you say?' said Peets with hope in his heart.

'There is another portal that I am aware of on this planet. That one is most definitely not guarded by the humans.' Koro said quietly.

'How do you know Koro?' Exclaimed Peets daring to hope.

'It is not guarded by the Humans as it is situated in the lava tubes,' continued the bear. 'And the humans do not control the lava tubes on this planet. They tried to take them and they failed. The Mantis control them.'

'The Mantis?' Asked Peets. 'What are they?'

'They are an insectoid creature which have inhabited this planet for as far back as it is known. They are very territorial and they have always lived in the lava tubes. The humans tried to get rid of them when they first arrived here but lost many lives in this futile battle. The Mantis would never give up the tubes. They would never give them up as they are a safe haven underground from any debris that comes flying into the Solar system. And they will also not give them up as they know what lies in there. A portal. A gateway off the planet.'

Peets felt the hope in his heart soar. 'Well what are we waiting for?' He shouted. 'Let's go, let's go to the lava tubes! You know the Mantis right? You can ask them if they will let me use the portal to go home?' The excited little Sasquatch almost ran out of the cave.

'Wait Peets,' said Koro calmly. 'We have to do something else first before we can go to the lava tubes.'

Peets turned to look at his shaggy friend. 'What, what else do we need to do?'

'We need to find out *when* the portal will take you back to where you want to go.' Explained Koro patiently.

'Delavia?' Peets said understanding what Koro was getting at. 'We need to find out *when* the portal that is in the lava tubes, is aligned to go back to Delavia? As if I get in it at any other time, it will take me back to somewhere other than Delavia? Like what happened today?' Peets exclaimed sheepishly.

'Yes my friend,' smiled Koro. 'That is correct. You are starting to learn.'

Peets frowned and felt sad. How he wished he had taken the time to think about that before he had ended up on Mars. He should not have just rushed into the portal. He should have waited for Father. All he could do now was try and get back home to Delavia. 'How will I find out when the portal goes back to Delavia Koro?' Asked Peets, wondering how it all worked. He wanted to get back as fast as he could.

'We have to obtain the Ancient portal map which shows the alignment of Mars to other planets electromagnetically. From that we can see when the portal in the lava tubes here on Mars, will be open towards Delavia. For you to travel to other planets through portals, the planet you are on has to be in a geometrical alignment to the planet that you are travelling to. Only then will you get to where you are wanting to go.' Explained Koro as he started to walk slowly into the darkness of the cave.

Peets ran to catch him up. He wished he could understand what the huge shaggy bear was saying, but he just couldn't quite grasp it. He had never heard of 'electromagnetically' or 'geometrical alignment' before. This was language that just wasn't used on Delavia.

'Who has the portal map Koro? We need to find it quickly! The quicker I can get back to Delavia, the quicker I can get Mother and Sneets to safety and find out if Father has made it back yet!'

'There is only one portal map that I am aware of on Mars,' explained Koro as they walked into the darkness, 'and it is controlled by the Cockroaches. We must go and barter with them.'

Cockroaches? Thought Peets. What are Cockroaches?

Lunar Operation Command

Isadora stepped slowly out of the ship and down onto the surface of the Moon. This was surreal. It really was hard to wrap your head around. Isadora had looked up in the sky and seen the Moon all her life. She had learnt about it in school. She had looked through her telescope with her Daddy at it when she was younger. And now she was stood on it. Neil Armstrong's voice popped into her head and a little bubble of excitement shot up from her stomach. One small step for Isadora she thought. One giant leap for womankind. As she stepped forwards she watched as her footsteps stayed within the chalkiness of the Moon's surface. It was fascinating. She looked back up as she could sense that Kaia was storming off into the distance and making her way towards the Lunar Operation Command building. I must not fall behind Isadora thought. But there is so much to see!

As they got nearer to the LOC Building, Isadora started to feel really excited. Her thoughts flicked to her Momma at home on Earth. I guess this is kind of like a Geography trip she smiled inside. Only Geography on another planet! Here I am stepping across a rocky terrain. I could be doing that on a Geography trip she mused. What rocks did you study on your Geography trip Isadora? She imagined her Momma asking her. Oh just Moon rocks Momma, she laughed inside. She tripped over a jagged rock and nearly fell. Orion turned round to help her. I must concentrate on what I'm doing she thought only this is all so surreal I think I'm losing my mind. Maybe it's the lack of gravity?

'It's definitely the lack of gravity Isadora!' Said Orion's voice in her head laughing. 'And it's not every day a girl gets to go to the Moon right?'

I should really practice that white shield around my mind Isadora laughed as she looked at Orion. He's always right there in my mind. Isadora smiled and gave Orion a little shove. Orion smiled back, his huge white dazzling smile. And he pushed her right back. She bounced up into the air. Wow this feels incredible she thought as her feet left the Moon slowly and gracefully. As she landed she saw that Kaia was stood at the front of the building which was built into the face of the rocks. Kaia was waiting patiently to see that all of her party had caught up. She had a disapproving look on her face as if she was annoyed at Isadora and Orion messing around. Isadora stopped smiling and tried to look serious. They were here to help Chinga. His family were at risk. Not mess around shoving each other in zero gravity. It sure felt good though she thought. The feeling of weightlessness. Freedom.

Hyperion's ship had landed and Isadora could see them all filling off. Her eyes searched for Adama. He was taller than all the rest. Isadora's heart leapt. Maybe I'll get chance to speak to him again when we get inside? She thought excitedly. Kaia was satisfied that everyone was here and turned to the building. She looked into a retinal scanner on the front of the building and the door opened. Isadora felt sick. She was walking into a building which was on the Moon. This was crazy. They all stepped slowly inside.

Isadora looked around in disbelief. Inside this high tech building on the Moon. It just looked like an old school from something like the 50's. All the décor inside was really old fashioned. Where was all the Sci Fi stuff? This can't be right she thought? You'd think that they would have better Technology on THE MOON than this? Why did it look like an old school that was in desperate need of repair? Kaia had read Isadora's thoughts and responded with a laugh. 'The Moon is an extraordinary place Isadora. From the surface this building looks very small built into the rock. But the real surprise is under the surface. For this building goes deep within the centre of the Moon and there are many many levels to this facility. The level we are on now is just for the people with low level access to come and go from. Where we are going to now. You have to have really high security clearance to get access to. Luckily you are with me. Also how's that white light shield coming on?' Kaia teased. Isadora blushed and she started trying to practice putting white light around her mind.

Hyperion's crew had caught them up on the walk through the building and General Myers shouted across the party of people. 'Agarthans people! I am going down now to fetch our reinforcements. I will load them on the craft and then wait there for your signal that we are good to go to Delavia.'

Hyperion and Kaia both frowned. Isadora wasn't sure if this was because General Myers had called them Agarthans People. Or if it was because it appeared as if he was trying to take over when Hyperion was the commander of his ship. Or if it was just because General Myers' demeanor was so rude and rubbed everybody up the wrong way. To be fair thought Isadora it could be any of those reasons. He was pretty much totally obnoxious. Kaia responded to the General in a pleasant tone. 'No problem General Myers. We are going down to the lower levels to fetch something also and I will signal to Hyperion once we are back in the ship that we are ready to travel to Delavia.'

General Myers grimaced in response. He clearly hated taking direction from a woman. Isadora noticed that General Myers was stood in front of a different elevator to the one that they were stood in front of. And that he seemed to know where he was going. He must have been here a few times before. She also noticed wistfully that Adama was stood with General Myers so she would not have the opportunity to talk to him again it would seem for a while. She risked looking at him. Although she wouldn't look very attractive at the moment with the gear that she had on. He wasn't looking in her direction anyway. Her palms felt sweaty. Could they take this thing off now?

Their elevator opened. Kaia and Isadora's party stepped into the elevator. As the elevator door started to slowly close, Isadora risked a look at Adama again. This time he was looking. They both smiled at each other at the same time. Isadora's heart started beating faster in her chest. It felt like electricity was passing between them. Like this moment would last forever. Then the elevator doors shut and Adama was gone. They were travelling fast, very fast. Deeper and deeper down into the Moon. How far down were they going? What was down there? I guess we're about to find out thought Isadora and steeled herself.

The Journey

Peets was tired. He couldn't remember the last time he had slept. His legs were tired. His eyes were tired. Even the soles of his feet were tired. But he couldn't give up he had to carry on. Peets and Koro had walked for miles into the darkness of the caves on Mars. The general direction which they seemed to be heading was down. The temperature was getting slowly colder and colder and Peets had started to shiver. During the journey his eyes had adjusted to the dark as there seemed to be some curious luminescent plants which lived in these underground caves. They were beautiful and gave off a level of light. It was just enough that it illuminated their way and they could see where they were going.

'How much longer will it be Koro? Are we nearly where the Cockroaches live?' Peets asked the shaggy bear hoping really hard that they were nearly there.

'Not too much longer my little friend.' Reassured the bear. 'Can you see the dim light in the distance?'

Peets squinted, 'Yes, yes I can. Is that where they are?'

'Yes,' said Koro. 'That is where they live. When we get there, let me do the talking. They will not listen to you as you are not from here. Cockroaches are selfish beings and only think of themselves. They will do anything to survive at the mercy of everything. It is why they have survived for so long. Let me do the talking and I will negotiate with them.'

'OK,' said Peets. 'How are you going to negotiate with them? What will they want? What are you able to give?'

Koro let out a sigh, a really long sigh which sounded like he had been holding that breath for a really really long time. 'I am not sure yet little one. There are a few things that I have which I may be able to barter with to access you what you need. But there is one thing above all which the Cockroaches value, and that is land.'

'Land?' Cried Peets. 'What do you mean Koro? Land like where you live?' Peets started to think. He couldn't let Koro give away anything of his. Not for him it wasn't fair. We have lots of underground caves on Delavia thought Peets as he relived sending his people off to hide in them. We never normally use them for anything really. We Delavian's prefer to live out in nature and in the light, surrounded by trees. 'Maybe we could use the Delavian caves as something to barter with?' Said the little creature. 'I'm sure none of the Delavians would mind as we never normally use them?'

'We shall see little one.' Said the big bear. 'The last thing you want is your planet over run with giant Cockroaches. Best they stay here than spread still further and take over another world. I shall see if what I have to barter is acceptable to them first. We are nearly here. Remember what I said to you, let me do the talking.'

Peets looked up at the huge bear and felt very lucky to have made such a wonderful friend out of such a terrible experience. 'Yes Koro I will. I won't say a peep.'

'Good little one, best leave it to me.' And the two stepped forward around the corner of the cave tunnel and into the murky light of beyond.

The Weapon

The elevator had been travelling down into the inside of the Moon for what had seemed like forever. How deep does this thing go thought Isadora? Is it hollow? What were they going to fetch anyway? Had Kaia mentioned what they were going to fetch? She couldn't remember. So much had happened. It was hard to get your head around a lot of what had happened over the past few days. She sensed that what they were going to fetch was important but she didn't know why.

Kaia smiled at Isadora. 'You are right Isadora!' She said her eyes dancing. 'What we are going to fetch is of grave importance. The success of our mission rests upon it. I truly, truly hope that when we reach Delavia, Valdazar and his army will surrender peacefully. We have many tricks up our sleeve in order to broker peace. However Valdazar is of the dark forces. He does not care for life. He does not care that life has a choice. He does not care that it is not the choice of the Delavian peoples to be captured and kept as prisoner. All Valdazar cares about is power. Power, greed and control. That is the way of the dark. The Agarthans and many other beings are the way of the light. We have something that Valdazar does not have and that is Thor's Hammer. This is a piece of Technology that only works for the light. It will rid all places and all worlds of the darkness, if the darkness will not peacefully come back to the light. If Valdazar will not surrender, then we may have to use this Technology to free our Delavian friends. Keep working on that shield Isadora.' Kaia reminded.

Isadora thought she must have mis-heard Kaia. 'I'm sorry Kaia. Did you just say 'Thor's Hammer? Isn't that something from a film?' Isadora was confused. 'Like make believe? It's just something that they use in a film isn't it? With that Chris guy?' Isadora concentrated hard. No she couldn't remember his name. His Brother was dating Miley Cyrus though and she thought he might have been in Hunger Games.

Kaia smiled. 'This is what is wrong with you surface humans Isadora.' She said kindly touching Isadora's face. 'You believe everything that you see in the movies to be fake or make believe. Yet everything that your politicians say to be true. And why is this? Through no fault of your own. You are conditioned in this way from birth. Your parents were conditioned in this way from birth and their parents before them.' Sadness crept over Kaia's face and Isadora could see tears fill her eyes. 'You never stood a chance against their deceit and lies. They have controlled you for generations and none of you are aware of just how powerful you are and what you can and could do if you were fully aware of your power. It is time that you surface humans took your power back. Stand up to the liars and cheats who control your world. Demand to know the answers.' Kaia's voice trailed off as the elevator stopped and indicated that they had reached their destination.

What the hell was Kaia talking about? Thor's Hammer was real? What was she trying to say? Isadora had that same sick feeling in the pit of her tummy where something new and startling was about to be revealed. Her consciousness started to brush it off as Kaia just being weird, but something started to resonate with Isadora. Somehow she knew that Kaia was telling her the truth. She 'felt' that she was. But the confusion of that was almost too much to bear. First Adama, now Kaia telling her that 'surface humans' didn't know what was going on. What did it all mean?

Isadora's thoughts were broken by the sound of the elevator opening and everyone letting out a gasp of air. The bright divine light of the room that the elevator had just opened into cascaded into the elevator with such a force that Isadora stumbled backwards into the elevator and crashed into Orion. He caught her before she fell to the floor. What was in that room?

Orion lifted Isadora back up so slowly and carefully as if she was made of glass, and placed her carefully back on her feet. There was so much kindness in his face. Isadora had only known him a matter of days, yet she felt like she had known him all her life.

'Thanks Orion,' Isadora smiled.

'No problem Ma'am,' said the gorgeous Cowboy and gave her a dazzling smile.

Kaia stepped into the bright whiteness of the room and out of the elevator and all the rest of her crew followed.

'Wow!' Exclaimed Chinga who up to this point had been very quiet. He was clearly worried about his family and had gone inside himself.

There in the middle of a huge white room, suspended in mid-air, was a huge hammer. It glistened and shimmered. Electrical currents crackled and popped all around it. It was silvery, light. The purest, whitest light Isadora had ever seen. Beautiful. The energy emanating from the room was incredible and Isadora felt happier than she had ever felt in the 15 years of her life. They were stood in front of something very special, very magical. Thor's Hammer. Just like in the movies. Only this was real. And it was mesmerising.

'Well I'll be damned.' Thought Isadora stunned.

Kaia laughed.

The Cockroaches

Peets and Koro were currently stood in front of the King of the Cockroaches. Peets was doing his best not to be sick. He did not want to appear rude. But the Cockroaches really, really stunk. Peets wasn't sure what the smell was but he had never smelt anything like it in his life before. If he didn't really need this portal map to help him time his way back home correctly, he would not still be stood here. Koro did not seem to be affected by it, or if he was he didn't show it. Peets had not said a word as instructed by Koro ever since they had been led down the winding passageways. Led further into the depths of the deep, dank caves. To meet the King of the Cockroaches. Koro was well known here it would seem and as soon as he had met with one of the soldier Cockroaches, they had been led straight to the King. Peets really hoped that this meant that he would soon be on his way home. The King of the Cockroaches was huge. The soldier Cockroaches themselves were easily as tall as a full grown Sasquatch and the King was double the size of the soldier Cockroaches. He scared Peets a lot. But he was trying very hard to be brave. And not be sick.

'Sylas my old friend!' Said Koro nodding to the King of the Cockroaches. 'I come here today to ask of you a favour.'

'A favour?' Spoke the huge Cockroach telepathically into the two companions heads. 'What can I possibly have that would be of interest to you Koro.' From the tone of both Koro and Sylas' voices, and also from the vibes coming from each creature. Peets could tell that Koro and Sylas did not like each other very much and they were definitely not friends.

'You will see with me that I have a companion here,' continued the bear. 'My friend Peets is a Sasquatch from the planet Delavia. He has ended up on this planet in error and he is looking to get back to Delavia and to his Mother and Father as soon as possible.'

The huge Cockroach realised he had the upper hand and slowly smiled an evil smile. Showing the most disgusting mouth Peets had ever seen. 'And you want my portal map to show you *when* he needs to travel home?' The King Cockroach sat back on his throne which was made of what looked to be some sort of twisted vines and laughed, a long evil laugh. 'And what is in it for me Koro? What do I get in exchange for letting this creature borrow my most prized possession?'

Peets was about to talk but then remembered what Koro had said about letting him negotiate. So he remained quiet as previously instructed.

Koro took a deep breath and began talking. 'After we borrow your map, we will be going to the Mantis to request access to the lava tubes where as you know the portal is housed. I will also have to give them something too in exchange for the access to the portal in the tubes that are controlled by them. I am proposing that I give you both the same thing.'

'Really?' Sneered the large Cockroach. 'And what would that be Koro? What would I want that the Mantis would want too?' He leaned forward on his throne, clearly interested in what the bear had to say.

Peets looked at Koro wondering where this was going.

'You know that it has long been the desire of us indigenous creatures here on Mars to take back what the humans have taken from us.' The bear began.

Sylas frowned. This didn't seem to sit well with him as the Cockroaches had arrived at the same time as the humans did. Within their boxes and boxes of supplies shipped up from Earth. Due to the difference in atmosphere and gravity on Mars, the Cockroaches had quickly been able to grow to much larger proportions on this planet. It also helped that there were a lot more places for them to hide and not as many humans to hunt them down and kill them. Even so, their negative memories of the humans from their time spent with them on Earth were still imprinted on the Cockroaches minds. Koro was right, the Cockroaches hated the humans just as much as the Bears did. These particular humans anyway. The ones who were in control. The humans that were incarcerated by their own kind, the Cockroaches felt sorry for. They were just slaves. They didn't even have as much freedom as the Cockroaches did. What they did have though, was volume. There were hundreds of the incarcerated humans and only maybe 20 of the ones who were in control, stationed here on Mars. Sylas thought about what the humans had done to this planet since they had all come here and he admitted if they allowed them to carry on in the way they had been doing, they would eventually take over. Humans, or at least the dominant ones, seemed to have an uncontrollable desire to take over and conquer everything and had no respect for other life forms. They would not be happy until they had destroyed everything. And even then, Sylas doubted that would make them happy. Sylas knew that at some point his people would be reduced to running from the humans again for fear of being squashed. Albeit they would have a tough time 'squashing' them now. As in the altered gravity of Mars, the Cockroaches had been able to grow far, far bigger than humans. In that moment he made up his mind to listen to what the bear had to say.

'Go on.' Said the huge Cockroach magnanimously.

Looking slightly relieved Koro continued. 'The humans that are in control are evil. They even incarcerate and treat their own kind as slaves. What will they do to us when the time comes that they decide they want our land too? Eventually they will start expanding and there will be no place safe soon for us to reside. We need to find a way to defeat them. And the only way we are going to do that is if we find out as much as we can about them. Find out what their weaknesses are. So we are able to overthrow them and take our planet back.'

'And how are we going to do that?' Sneered the large Cockroach clearly interested in what Koro would say next.

Koro turned to look at Peets. Peets gulped. 'That's where our little friend here comes in.' Said the huge bear with a smile on his face. 'He's that cute, they're bound to open up to him.' Koro started to laugh at Peets' aggrieved expression. Sylas had a look of revulsion on his face as if he had no idea what cute meant.

'But Koro,' said the small Sasquatch. 'If they won't listen to you and you're a huge bear. Why would they listen to me when I'm just a small boy? Besides, you said they were evil? What happens if they do something to me?'

'The boys right,' agreed the Cockroach King looking slightly dismayed. 'They won't even let him get to the gates. They'll kill him soon as look at him.'

'I'm not talking about the evil ones,' smiled Koro. 'I'm talking about the ones in captivity.'

The Cockroach King stared blankly at Koro for what seemed like an age. Then he started to laugh. At first Peets thought he was choking but no he was definitely laughing. 'Ha Ha Ha! That's brilliant!' Snorted Sylas. 'Truly brilliant my friend. You're going to use *this one*,' said the King pointing to Peets.' To befriend the captured ones. To get access to the ones in control. And then overthrow them! I love it, it's a great plan. And who knows,' said the Cockroach King. 'It may even work. He leaned into Koro with a look of pure glee on his face. So how are we going to do it?'

Koro smiled, 'Our little friend here, the colour of his fur, is the exact same colour of the terrain here. If we get him in position near the far side perimeter fence at night when they are not paying attention. Then he will be IN position when the captives come out for their morning break.'

Koro turned to speak directly to Peets. 'The captured ones are let out to stretch their legs twice a day. Once in a morning and once in the afternoon. They come out into a huge pen which has fencing all around to keep them in and barbed wire on top of that. At the end of the pen, the guards will not be able to see you conversing with any of the captured humans due to the colour of your fur. I suggest you try and strike up a conversation with somebody and use your choice wisely as we do not want our plan being exposed to the ones in power. Strike up a friendship with one of them and then find out what you can in terms of their weapons inside the facility, their control features inside the facility. Meal times, sleep times, how many guards there are, when they sleep etc. Find out as much as you can and we will do the rest.'

The Cockroach King smiled at Koro, 'So this is what you have to offer me then Koro in return for some time with my portal map? Possible Planet Liberation of the scourge that is Human?' He sat back in his chair and pondered.

Peets held his breath. So too did Koro.

'OK,' said the Cockroach King smiling. 'Let's do it.'

The Clones

Kaia strode into the room and reverently and gracefully moved Thor's Hammer into a silver metallic bag that glistened like it was made of liquid. As soon as Kaia had transferred the hammer into the strange bag, all of the light was totally extinguished from the room. It was incredible. The hammer emitted so much light that they were all still squinting. Kaia jumped back into the elevator and now they were travelling back up from whence they had come. Isadora was staring at the bag that was in Kaia's hand with fascination and trying desperately to remember the plotline of that film with Thor's Hammer in it. Why hadn't she paid more attention! Well she didn't realise at the time that it was going to turn out to be real that's why! That's crazy! Isadora's mind started to whirl. So Thor's Hammer was real? Does that mean that all films are real? Why are films real? Why don't normal humans know this? What are normal humans?

Kaia turned to look at her 'Isadora, keep practicing that mind shield I have described to you. I will give you answers to all of your questions in time. But right now we do not have 'time'. We have to save our friend here's family.'

Isadora felt shame flush over her face in a wave of red. She'd been that busy thinking about herself that she had never thought about Chinga's family at all. Not once ever since they had boarded the spaceship. She felt terrible. She hadn't even asked him if he was doing ok.

Chinga hearing her thoughts leaned in to hug his friend. 'It's OK my friend,' whispered the large Sasquatch. 'I'm doing enough worrying for the both of us.' Chinga's eyes swam with tears and he put a hand over his heart almost as if the pain was too much. 'I never should have left my family, not for one moment. Family is everything. We don't need the Honey. We never did.'

Isadora's heart broke for her friend. She felt his pain. She knew the pain of losing a loved one. Her Daddy was never far from her thoughts. She hugged Chinga tight hoping that somehow that would make him feel better.

Suddenly the elevator stopped and the doors opened. Isadora looked up to see what the noise was, it was deafening. 'LEFT, RIGHT, LEFT RIGHT!' Screamed General Myers voice.

Isadora could not believe her eyes. Rows and rows of soldiers were marching out of the LOC and towards the spaceships. There were literally hundreds. Surely they didn't need this many soldiers Isadora thought? She was aware that Kaia was hopeful that they would be able to negotiate Delavia back peacefully. So why did they need all of this Military might? Isadora looked at the soldiers trudging by in an endless stream. When suddenly she became aware of the fact that they all had the same face. She felt sick. Why did they all look the same? They looked human, completely human. She was pretty close to them as she was near the edge of the elevator and she could see that they all had the same face. Even down to a large mole that was on the right cheek of every one. She looked at Orion for reassurance. Orion nodded back at her with concern on his face. 'Yes,' the handsome Cowboy said into her head. 'You have noticed, they are Clones. It's the easiest way to save the needless ending of human life. There are often a lot of casualties in space wars, so we normally use Clones to prevent the loss of human souls. We have Technology that can replicate a complete person. Even taking their consciousness and training and replicating that. So basically what you got there, pointed Orion at the endless stream of soldiers, is the best, most elite soldier that we have ever trained, replicated a thousand times. The perfect army. We often use Clones in space wars, its normal.'

Normal? Thought Isadora, starting to feel numb. Hell what was normal? She'd be damned if she knew.

David

Peets' back was aching, really aching. He had been here for what had seemed like forever. His consciousness reminded him why he was here and he found new strength to fortify his resolve. 'You should have stayed with Mother and Sneets. You should not have run off to look for Father. Mother and Sneets needed you to stay and protect them. What happens if the Valdons had already woken up and Mother and Sneets have been harmed?' Peets felt sick. The shame and anger that he felt at himself and the decision that he had made was so strong that he almost started crying. However he steeled himself. If he ever wanted a chance to see his Mother, Father and Sister again. He was going to have to be successful at obtaining this information from the humans, to give to the Cockroaches and the Mantis. Suddenly it occurred to Peets that he didn't really know what humans looked like. How would he know which ones were the good guys and which ones were the bad guys? He would just have to see if he could 'read' them and make the right choice.

He was as Koro had instructed at the very end of the exercise yard, on the opposite side of the wire fencing that kept the humans penned in. He was curled up in a ball and the colour of his fur blended right in with the terrain of Mars. It was uncanny, and also very lucky he thought! He had no idea what time it was but it had been light for quite a while. Surely it had to be break time soon. Suddenly a loud noise which sounded much like a horn rang out over the massive expanse of empty terrain. It made Peets jump so hard his teeth started to chatter. A huge door to the human compound started to open. Peets rolled onto his side to get a better look. Adrenaline coursed through his little body. He wanted to get up and run. Run far away. But her couldn't. If he wanted to get home he had to stay here and be-friend one of these incarcerated humans. This was his only shot at seeing his family again. Peets took some slow, long deep breaths to calm down.

The humans began to file out into the outside exercise area. They were in two lines and walked out two by two. There must have been a few hundred of them Peets thought when the last pair filed out and the compound door began to shut. Peets looked at these funny beings. They didn't have hair all over their body like him. They just had hair on top of their head. How strange! They had no fur at all on their bodies. And they wore things on their bodies to cover up their nakedness. These garments were grey in colour and looked pretty dirty. Suddenly Peets realised what it was that seemed so familiar to him about them. They were the same beings as Valdazar. Peets began to feel angry. He HATED Valdazar. And these humans were the same as him! Peets' chest heaved up and down as he tried to calm himself down. The humans slowly and cautiously started to break off into little groups. They seemed very scared and afraid at first to talk to each other. As far as Peets could tell there was only one guard outside and he was sat in a tower that overlooked the whole of the exercise yard. He would be able to see if anyone tried to climb the wire fencing. He was also armed with a gun.

From how cautiously the humans were acting, Peets could sense that they dare not try to escape any more as this had been tried countless times and failed. They would just be shot. Peets continued to watch the humans who were incarcerated. He felt really, really sorry for them. Their spirits had been broken. He could tell. They looked unhappy. He was watching a family interact with each other. A Father and Mother were breaking off to hug their children, but they did so fretfully as if they feared that they might be taken from them at any moment. The children looked so happy to be able to hug their Mother and Father. But they all seemed broken, like the fight had been knocked out of them.

Peets felt tears streaming down his fur. What had happened to these people? Why were they being held captive by their own kind? He always thought that you looked after your own people? That you should look after all beings, even those that were not the same as you? Every being was a part of the one true creator. The one source that is the source of all. Yet these humans did not even look after all of their own kind? What evil was at work here? It was obviously a trait with humans. You were either really evil like Valdazar and these ones here, who kept their people captive. Or you were good. But it looked like the good ones were controlled by the bad ones? What made the good ones good? Even though they were being treated so appallingly by their masters? Peets just didn't understand it at all but he did not have time to understand it. He had to quickly pick someone to try and talk to. His eyes swept across the many humans that were milling around the exercise yard. Then suddenly his eyes were drawn to a little boy.

There was a little boy who was on his own. He didn't have anyone with him. He looked really sad. Peets watched him closely. The little boy looked fretful, tired and sad. He had no one with him at all. He was purposely working his way to the back of the exercise yard. He was more or less walking directly to where Peets was curled up in a ball on his side and watching. He looked to be no more than 7 or 8 years old. As he was walking towards the back of the exercise complex. Peets saw him put his hand inside the grubby, flimsy covering that was on his body. His thin little arm brought something out of his covering. It looked like a piece of paper. As the boy got closer to where Peets was, Peets could tell that the piece of paper was a picture of some kind. The boy just made it to the end of the exercise yard and was almost directly above Peets' head when he let out a gasp and his entire body shook.

Peets looked up at the small, thin boy. His chest was heaving. Suddenly Peets realised, the boy was crying but he was trying to keep quiet. Presumably so he didn't attract the attention of the guard. The boy gasped and gasped as if he couldn't get enough air into his lungs and tears streamed down his little face. He clutched hold of his heart as if it might burst. Peets sat and watched the boy in respectful silence. He felt that he was witnessing something that he shouldn't be and he did not want to interrupt. The boy was very upset and all Peets wanted to do was reach out and hug him, and tell him that everything would be ok. That he would help him. But even as Peets thought these words, he could sense from the deep emotion coming from the boy that this little boy's world would never be the same again. They had taken something from him. But what? Peets thought. He listened with his heart and he heard. He felt in his heart that they had taken this little boy's parents away. The paper he was holding and clutching onto as if it was the most precious thing in the world to him, was a picture of his parents.

Peets suddenly realised how important it was to help these people. They were innocent victims, just like his fellow Delavians were. Although these too were humans, they were different to Valdazar and the ones who were in control here. Their *energy* was different. Peets could feel it. These people were good. And they needed his help. As the little boy sobbed quiet, desperate sobs, seemingly unnoticed by his own kind, Peets made a decision. His going home could wait. He still had a Mother and a Father and a Sister. This little boy had no one. He was completely alone in the world. This little boy's Mother and Father had been taken away from him, and so therefore had his childhood. That was not acceptable. Peets knew what the right thing was to do. His Father had always taught him that the right thing was always to help others. 'If you can help Peets, so you must,' was one of his Fathers favourite sayings. 'I can help Father, so I must,' said the little Sasquatch inside his head. As the little boys sobs slowly subsided and he slumped onto the floor, Peets sucked up all his courage. He stayed curled up in a ball so as not to shock the little boy too much, but he opened his mouth and spoke.

'Hello my friend,' said Peets really softly and quietly. 'I am here to help you. I will help you escape.'

The little boy jumped, but instantly a huge smile spread over his face.

'He listened!' the boy whispered in wonder.

'Who listened?' asked Peets in confusion.

'God, I asked him for a miracle. I asked him to help me avenge my parents death and to set us all free. I asked him to send me someone who could help. And you are here, you're really here!' Laughed the little boy wiping the snot from his nose.

Peets smiled, he knew he had done the right thing. 'The one true creator will always listen to your prayers my friend!' Said the little Sasquatch.

'Now here's what we're going to do...'

Saving Delavia

The last of the Clone soldiers had just filed past Isadora and her party on the elevator. They were now able to exit the LOC and make their way back to the ships. As they exited the LOC and back out onto the surface of the Moon, Isadora could see General Myers shouting at the last of the Clones to embark onto his ship. Hyperion was stood next to General Myers frowning. It was very obvious to anyone with eyes that Hyperion was not happy at all about General Myers ordering everyone around. He was the captain of that ship. There was a definite struggle for power going on there thought Isadora. Suddenly Isadora was aware of Adama coming towards her. She really wished she wasn't in this ridiculous spacesuit.

'What did you think to the Clones?' Said Adama smiling. 'It's always a bit strange when you see Clones for the first time.'

'Yeah, ahhhh, they're *really* weird!' Laughed Isadora. 'Like seeing all of those people with the same face. It was just weird.'

Adama laughed, and his eyes danced. 'If you think that is weird, wait till you see the Clones of some of your famous surface humans on Earth.' The gorgeous young man laughed.

'What do you mean Adama?' Asked Isadora in shock. He had to be joking right?

'Most of your famous people and world leaders have Clones Isadora,' laughed Adama. 'Mostly for safety reasons. If a clone gets shot whilst giving a speech, it doesn't matter right? Because it's just a clone? But also for longevity reasons. Some of these tours these famous people do. How do you think they perform every night? Night after night after night? How do their voices not give out? How do their bodies not give out? Clones!' Adama looked at her with a smile on his face waiting for her reaction.

'I don't understand,' said Isadora going red. 'Adama was so much more intelligent than her, he had to think she was so stupid. She didn't know anything. She thought for a moment trying to process what Adama had just told her and continued. So you're saying that most famous people and world leaders have Clones?'

'Adama!' Shouted Tiamut. His voice had an angry tone to it. It made both Adama and Isadora jump as he had shouted so loud. 'Get into your ship please, we need to go.' Barked Adama's Father crossly.

Adama looked at the floor embarrassed, 'Yes Father,' he replied quietly and began walking off to the ship.

Tiamut walked over to Isadora and started to guide her back to the ship that they had landed in.

'My Son is promised to another,' Tiamut whispered under his breath as he gripped tightly onto her arm. 'The Agarthans are not allowed to fraternize with any other beings. We are pure. A union between an Agarthan and a surface human would never be allowed. Whatever feelings you have for my Son. Whatever you hoped would happen. Please forget it Isadora. It will never be permitted.'

Isadora looked up at Tiamut and could tell that he had conflicting emotions. He liked her but she wasn't good enough for his Son. She got it. She didn't know half as much as the Agarthans did. They all probably thought she was stupid. A stupid, naive surface human.

She pulled away from Tiamut's grip. 'Its fine Tiamut, don't worry, I don't have designs on your Son. I have far more important things to attend to like helping free my friends family.'

She strode away from Tiamut and climbed onto the ship.

As the ship gradually lifted and she said good bye to the Moon, tears started to flow down her cheeks. She cried for everything. She cried for a Daddy that she would never see again. She cried for a Momma who had never been the same since her Daddy had disappeared. She cried for the fact that she was so confused. She had learnt so much over the past few days and it was so overwhelming.

She was just a normal American girl trying to get through life. Why had she been given these 'gifts' that made her so abnormal? She didn't fit in anywhere. She didn't fit in with anyone at school as she was so different. And she didn't fit in with anyone here on this ship as she was just a surface human.

She missed her Daddy so much.

She missed her Momma so much

As the hot angry tears started to fall.

And her chest felt like it was bursting.

She cried for Adama and a dream that was lost.

Sneets

Sneets was trying to comfort her Mother but she would not stop crying.

'Mother we have to leave the Valdons will wake soon! We have to get back to the caves and hide there until Father gets back to save us!'

Sneets tried really hard to pull her Mother up from the floor but she would not move.

'Once Father is back we can then go and find Peets!' Cried Sneets. 'But if the Valdons wake up and kill us then were not going to be able to go and find Peets OR Father, Mother listen *please*!'

Her Mother would not get up off of the floor. She was broken. She had lost her mate who had not come back. She knew this as if he was on Delavia she would be able to hear him telepathically and she couldn't. And now she had lost her little boy. She had failed at being a Mother. Her heart was in pieces.

Suddenly both Sneets and her Mother heard 'Hang in there my darlings I am coming. Can you hear me? Sneets, Peets, Lamay my love. Can you hear me? I am coming. We are coming. We will be with you soon.'

Sneets and her Mother looked at each other in shock and leapt into one another's arms. Both cried happy tears. That was Chinga! 'My Love!' Screamed Lamay. 'My love, my love, where are you?' She jumped up and started running out of the glade they were in to see if she could find him. Where was he? Where had his voice come from?

Suddenly two huge ships appeared in the early morning sky. They just appeared out of nowhere. One minute they weren't there, the next they were. They hung in the sky like two huge shimmering rays of hope.

'You've come to save us! Oh Chinga my love where are you? Are you on the big ships?' Screamed Lamay telepathically.

'Yes my darling I am on one of these ships. We are going to secure Valdazar's ship and then we will round up the Valdons. The Valdons have been drugged last night that's why they are still asleep. I have no idea how long they will stay that way for though. I want you to get to safety until we have contained the situation. Get off to the caves.'

'OK Chinga!' Replied Lamay waving to her mate. 'We will go now!' She smiled and waved up at the two big, shiny ships. Finally they were saved. Her heart soared with love and happiness.

Suddenly, just as Sneets and Lamay were turning to begin their walk to the caves. One of the two rescue ships shot a *huge* blast straight at Valdazars ship. The sound that ricocheted around the Delavian skies as the laser shot hit the huge black ship, was deafening. The gargantuan black, spikey ship exploded in an instant of the missile hitting, into a million pieces. Huge smouldering pieces of ship shot through the sky like fiery missiles and cascaded all over the floor as far as the eye could see. Fiery lumps of charred ship landed all over the forest floor like individual deadly weapons, maiming anyone that got in their way. The sleeping Valdons having been pelted by hundreds of lumps of charred and smouldering ship, began to lurch and wake up out of their deep, drunken slumbers. The huge Valdons began to scream as they realised that their clothes were on fire and disorientated, began dragging themselves to their feet. Running around in panic. Where had these two new ships come from? Where was Valdazars old ship? Was that what the big explosion was?

'Chinga!' Screamed Lamay in fright and shock, running for her life. 'Chinga! What is happening? You said we were safe? What is going on?'

The noise was deafening as the hundreds of pieces of exploded spaceship smashed into the forest floor on their decent. The ground shook as the remaining Valdons ran around desperately trying to stamp out the flames on the forest floor with their huge green, hairy feet. Whilst also patting themselves down as the angry flames danced around their putrid green, grotesque bodies. The Ancient ones had also been hit with the fiery debris and were trying as best as they could to pat out the flames on their bodies with their ineffectual, chubby arms.

As Sneets and Lamay ran for their lives in the direction of the tree canopy, gigantic fiery missiles landed all around them. Massive boulders of smouldering spaceship. Suddenly the sound of rapid laser fire peppered the air. Hyperion's ship was now open firing on the Valdons. The Valdons who were already scared, now started running around in mass panic looking for cover. Any cover which would camouflage their massive bodies from the lazer fire from above.

From the height of his ship, Chinga watched desperately as Lamay and Sneets ran for their lives. Fear gripped at his heart as he saw a monstrous Valdon hurtle towards the two of them as they ran towards the nearest canopy of trees. The Valdon had been hit in the back from the laser fire of Hyperion's ship. He fell to his knees, mortally wounded. As his massive, heavy lungs gave out, he gave a last guttural breath and his gargantuan body began to fall forwards. Forwards towards Lamay and Sneets.

Lamay and Sneets ran as fast as they could. Time stood still. Just a little bit further until they reached the safety and covering of the tree canopy. They heard the huge Valdon behind them, it sounded like he was falling. The last sound that Lamay heard from her husband as she willed her legs to go faster and she started to go dizzy from the lack of oxygen in her lungs, was Chinga's cry of desperation.

'Lamay my love, Sneets! Run faster. RUN!!!''Noooooooooooo!'

Betrayal

Valdazar had had his fill of meat and he was getting bored. He was waiting for the entertainment to arrive. He was having two of his prisoners brought up from the dungeons. He would give them both a weapon and let them fight to the death. And they would all take bets on which one they thought would survive. He loved this game. He loved it as he was very good at it. He always knew which one would win, it was a knack that he had.

As he was thinking about a previous fight that he had witnessed which he particularly loved, his clear smart pad started to blink and an image came up on it. He cast his eyes down at the image and suddenly rage and disbelief consumed his entire body. This could not be. How could this be? White hot fury trickled up his back and into his head. He picked up the small computer and squinted at it trying to make sense of what he was seeing.

'Sire, Sire!' Gurgled the dying Valdon on the screen. 'We have been taken. We have been..'

Valdazar watched as a gigantic ship appeared behind the Valdon and gunned down one of his prized warriors. There were explosions all over Delavia. He could see the rest of his Valdons either gunned down and lying dead on the floor or running for their lives. The screen went blank. Valdazar looked at the long table of Valdons who had just heard one of their comrades die a bloody death. They were all scared and stared at him in silence. They were looking to him for their next move.

Valdazar stood up and swiped all of the leftover food onto the floor. Silver platters clanged on the stone floor like angry rain drops. He threw his Smart Glass Pad across the room and narrowly missed garroting one of his own men.

As the Valdons cowered not knowing what their deranged master would do next, Valdazar howled. It was a blood curdling scream. One of rage, fear, anger and disbelief.

'How could this happen?!' Valdazar screamed incredulously. 'HOW!'

The General

Isadora was watching everything unfold in slow motion. This could not be happening she thought. How was this happening? Why was Hyperion's ship open firing on the Valdons? Why had they blown up Valdazar's ship? That was not the plan. They were supposed to be taken peacefully? Kaia was trying really hard to contact Hyperion telepathically but he was not answering. Chinga was screaming and trying to see out of the spaceship window that he and Isadora were on, to see if he could see his family. Were they OK? Did they make it? He had lost contact with them telepathically and he did not know why this was. Sometimes when you experience high levels of emotion or fear, contact can be lost so he was praying inside that this was what it was and his family were still safe. But he could not see them anymore and he was scared. Maybe they had made it to the canopy of trees? The huge, felled Valdon obscured his view.

'Kaia!' Screamed Chinga. 'What is going on? This was not the plan?! My mate and daughter could be killed? Why is this happening?'

'I do not know my friend!' Screamed Kaia with tears rolling down her beautiful, pale face. 'I cannot make telepathic contact with Hyperion. He has been compromised.' Kaia shouted all of this whilst trying to maneuver their ship around the erratic fire that was coming from Hyperion's ship. Hyperion's ship was all over the place. What was happening?

Fear coursed through Isadora's body. I hope Adama is OK on that ship? She had resigned herself to the fact that she couldn't be with him after being warned off by Tiamut. But she couldn't switch her feelings off for Adama that quickly. Why was Hyperion not following Kaia's orders?

Suddenly the rogue ship that Hyperion, General Myers and Adama were on started to descend and began to land on Delavia.

'What is he doing?' Screamed Kaia. Isadora was shaking she was so scared, if Kaia was losing her composure then they were in trouble.

They all watched in disbelief as the huge door on the rogue ship opened up and all of General Myers Clones spilled out onto Delavia. Hundreds of Clones filed out of the open spaceship door and dispassionately and methodically began to jump on any Valdons who had managed to survive thus far. The Clones vigorously began hacking at the huge Valdons and trying to pull them down onto the ground. As soon as they were on the ground the Clones effortlessly slit the Valdons throats. Isadora watched horrified. These Clones were just like machines. They had no compassion at all. She turned away and covered her eyes in shock. A clone who had managed to climb up a Valdon who was on his knees begging for his life, slowly smiled and plunged his knife into the crying Valdons throat. Isadora had never witnessed anything like this before in her life and it was horrifying.

Chinga screamed at Kaia, 'We have to get on that ship and find out what is going on! They are just randomly shooting or stabbing at anything on the ground. My mate and children might have been killed for all I know. What the hell is happening here?! I have to find my family. Please DO SOMETHING!'

Kaia nodded her face pale as snow. 'Yes, we will land the craft and you and I will try and get onto the other ship and take control. I fear that Hyperion is dead.' Kaia said her voice breaking. 'I cannot get contact with him.'

'I'm coming with you Ma-am,' said Orion. 'There's no way you are walking out there all guns blazing without me coming with you too.'

'Me too,' said Isadora. 'It's all for one right? And one for all.' She looked at Chinga, he looked fraught. He was desperate to find out what had happened to his family. The rest of the ships occupants nodded in agreement.

'OK, here we go.' said Kaia. She began to land the ship on an area of ground which thus far was unencumbered with dead Valdons.

'Follow me!' Shouted Kaia as she opened the ships door with her mind and they started to file off and into the deafening din of weapon fire and blood curdling screams.

As they stepped onto Delavia once more and Isadora took in the scene of the gigantic Valdons running for their lives and a sea of Military Clones killing everything that ran, Isadora couldn't help but think. What would Momma think?

Some Geography trip.

The Plan

Peets and David had talked for the whole time that the humans were allowed in the exercise yard. Peets had told David not to worry. That he would keep coming back to see him. And that he wasn't alone anymore. That he had friends who were helping him, and that they would come up with a plan to free him and his fellow captive humans. Peets explained to David that he would have to give him as much information as possible about how the compound worked so that they could formalise a full proof plan. He would take this information back to his friend Koro and they would in conjunction with the Cockroaches, come up with a plan to over throw the evil humans and help the good humans escape. Peets had even thought that if they could break the good humans out and they could negotiate with the Mantis to allow them access to the portal, then maybe the good humans could come back to Delavia with him? Delavia was massive and he was sure that his fellow Delavian people would be more than willing to help. Or if the humans didn't want to do that, they could have a brief respite on Delavia. Then Father could help them get back to the Honey planet which was where these humans had originally come from? Some of them according to David still had family members on the Honey planet.

David had explained to Peets that these family members thought the captive humans were dead. They had all been tricked you see. Years ago when these humans were brought to Mars, they had been told that Earth was about to be hit by a meteorite. That a huge meteorite was about to hit Earth and the majority of the human race would not survive. They had been told that the brightest minds on Earth and their immediate family members were being taken to Mars to ensure the continuation of the Human Race. And these humans had believed their leaders and had gone without hesitation. Not realising that the evil humans had for years had the Technology in place to destroy any meteorites that may have threatened Earths existence.

When they had gotten to Mars, they quickly realised that they had been duped. They had been tricked. They were not the brightest minds on Earth. They were the most stupid as they had allowed their ego's to 'buy in' to the idea that they were the *chosen ones*. They had got on the ships knowing that the rest of the human race that they had left behind, would be killed by the meteorite impact. Yet they had still left and not told a soul. They hadn't told the rest of humanity. They had kept quiet in order to save their own skins as they had been told that there was only room on the ships for a limited amount. If they told everyone it would start a panic. So had consoled themselves with the information that they were the chosen ones.

As soon as they got to Mars and they saw where they were supposed to be 'living' they sickeningly realised the true situation. There was no meteorite. There was no emergency situation. They had not been brought here to start a new colony of humans. They had been brought here by the 'evil ones' to be their worker bees in the Galaxy. And why not bring the most intelligent minds if you had the pick of everyone? They were devastated. They were angry. At first they tried to rise up and escape. Little groups of brave ones had tried to stand up to those in command, but they had no weapons and they were always killed. Over time, people didn't even try to stand up to them anymore. They just went along with their incarceration.

They went along with it as they felt that it was their own fault. They should not have been so arrogant and easy to leave their fellow humans on Earth to be wiped out. And because of their own shame at agreeing to this, they had believed ever since then that this was their punishment. That they deserved to be here and controlled. It made Peets so sad to hear David's story. Peets felt that David's people were good. They were good humans but they had just made wrong choices. What was even worse is that David himself had been born on Mars. He had never experienced any other life other than the unbearable one that he had now. The only sky he had ever seen was the dusty Mars sky from inside the exercise compound. He had never even seen the stars or the night sky as the evil humans never let them out at night. They were allowed out twice a day. Once in a morning and once in the afternoon. Peets would love to take David back to Delavia with him and let him see the beauty. The wildlife. The trees that sang to you. The flowers. It was breath taking.

David could not believe it. God had answered his prayers. And it had happened so quickly. That morning when he had walked across the exercise yard and he had breathed the air into his lungs, he had not wanted to be here anymore. The pain of living in a world where his parents were no longer here was too much to bear. He was only 7 years old. How was he supposed to continue through life without his Mother and Father? He just wanted to die and be with them.

They had come in the night two nights ago, when they were on lock down for bed. He had been half asleep and not known what was going on. His Father had resisted being taken but they had hit him on the head and knocked him out. He could still hear the screams of his Mother begging them to leave their Son alone. Him. 'We don't need *him*,' one of them had sneered. It was hard to see in the dark and David's eyes would not adjust quickly enough. But he had been able to make out through his sleep filled eyes, that they had put bags over his parents' heads. And then as quickly as they had arrived, they were gone. They had taken his parents.

Everyone had heard about the ones who come in the night. It happened many times. These people who were taken never came back. David did not know why they took them. He just knew that when you were taken, you never came back. And now they had come for his parents.

He had spent the rest of the night, sobbing. Scared. Crying out for his parents, even though he knew that he would never see them again. He had thought about taking his life, but he didn't really know how to do it. And he knew that his parents would be really upset with him if he did. They would want him to live. They would want him to fight. And now god had answered his prayers and he had a friend who would help him. The world didn't seem as scary now that he had a friend.

Peets had explained what he would need to do. Half of the time, David walked around with his eyes on the floor and never looked up. Trying to make himself look as small as possible so he would not be picked on. He was going to have to start taking notice of his surroundings. When were brake times? How many guards were there? What time was bed time? Where did the guards sleep? That sort of thing and give all that information to Peets so he and his friends could help them break free. Hopefully help them all break free. Peets had told David there was a way off this planet. Could it really be true? He allowed himself to hope. It had to be true as how had Peets gotten here otherwise? He was from another planet too!

David really, really hoped that Peets was telling the truth and that he would help him. He couldn't bare it if this were another trick.

But he knew, he felt it inside. This hairy creature was his friend and he would help him.
For the first time ever he felt a lightness enter his soul.
It was good to have friends.

Hyperion

Kaia was running towards Hyperion's ship, darting in and out of the fighting Valdons and Clones. Chinga, Orion and Isadora followed in pursuit. Isadora struggled to keep up. They were all so quick. I'm going to have to start trying a lot harder in gym she thought as her lungs threatened to burst.

Chinga broke off on route and shouted at his friends. 'I'm going to find my family, I will catch you up my friends!' And off he ran into the canopy of trees where he had last seen Lamay and his daughter.

Kaia, Orion, Isadora and the rest of the crew made it to Hyperion's ship and climbed up inside.

Isadora's heart leapt out of her chest as her eyes adjusted to the scene. Adama was currently wrestling with General Myers for control of a gun. Hyperion was lying motionless on the floor. Rala and Centaurus were also lying on the floor and not moving. Isadora felt sick. What could she do to help. She saw Kaia rush to Hyperion to see if he was still alive and attempt to move him out of the path of the grappling Adama and General Myers.

'Get off me you stupid alien!' Screamed General Myers in frustration and anger.

Adama was holding his own with General Myers but it looked like he was starting to tire. Tiamut was stood frozen, watching his Son in terror. He saw his Son starting to tire and screamed 'Not my Son!' Tiamut jumped forward and tried to help his Son in pulling the gun away from the Generals hands. The three men grappled for the weapon and the upper hand.

Everyone jumped as a shot rang out around the room.

Isadora held her breath. Please god no. Let Adama be OK she thought. Please, please let Adama be OK.

Suddenly Tiamut let out a huge gasp of air and collapsed on the floor. Horror spread across Adama's face as he realised that his Father had been shot.

'Father!' Adama screamed. 'Father! NOOOOOOOO!' Adama sank to his knees as he tried to help his Father.

General Myers stood behind Adama and let out a huge evil laugh. He pointed the gun at the back of Adama's head.

Isadora screamed 'Adama!'

Suddenly there was another shot, Isadora jumped out of her skin and her teeth started chattering. Who had been shot? Please god don't let it be Adama. But no, Adama was right there still attending to his Father.

The evil smile that was on General Myers face slowly turned to shock and disbelief. Out of the smoking bullet hole that was in his forehead, a trickle of blood slowly seeped out. The General fell backwards onto the floor. Dead.

Isadora turned to see where the shot had come from and saw Orion blowing the smoke from the end of his gun and spinning it around his finger before re-holstering his weapon.

He tipped his Cowboy hat at Isadora. 'I never did like that sum of a bitch!' The huge Cowboy said smiling. And he laughed really hard.

Isadora couldn't help but smile.

Lights Out

That night David lay in the dark alone. It was so strange to be in his little sleeping cell without his parents. They would always normally speak to each other in whispers before they fell to sleep. He still did the same tonight, but he had to imagine his parents' responses in his head. He thought about his new friend Peets. He was so lucky that Peets had come along. He really had hope that Peets and his friend Koro and the Cockroaches would be able to set his people free. He had done what Peets had said and he had started to take notice of things. How many guards there were. The guards names. Patterns of guards. How many on duty and when? He was starting to memorise everything.

Peets had said that he would meet him in the same place every day at morning break and he could pass the information onto him. Slowly when they had all the information that they needed, they would have enough to break them out. David held the hope of this to his chest like a shiny ball of light. To be free! I can't imagine what that would feel like he thought. The evil ones put him to work in the day. The one in charge of everything was called Eldon. He was pure evil. David worked in a factory that made spaceships. Well that's what was made when they put everything together. David himself just made one small part of the ships. Eldon and the evil humans traded these spaceships to other beings who sometimes landed on the planet. David knew this as some nights they were put in their cells earlier than others, straight after dinner. These were the nights that the 'beings' came. You could hear them walking down the halls with the guards. They spoke a different language to David and he couldn't understand them. But David thought that they sounded evil.

David's parents had explained to him under the cloak of darkness at night when they were tucked in their beds. That when they lived on Earth, before they had left to come to Mars. The Earth humans had no idea that the elite humans had reverse engineered alien space crafts from crafts that had crash landed on Earth. The average Earth human held a belief that humanity had only ever flown to the Moon and that this had been done in a rocket. When in actual fact, certain humans had really advanced spaceships and flew them all over our Galaxy and beyond. Up here on Mars, Eldon and his guards traded the spaceships that were made for other things that they wanted. David didn't know what that was. They were very careful not to tell any of the workers anything. David's parents were scientists. Before they were taken two nights ago, they would work in a lab day in and day out. Trying to invent new Technology and concepts for Eldon. David had thought that his parents would be safe as they were working on something very big for Eldon. That big that they wouldn't even tell him what they were working on in case someone kidnapped him and tortured him. Tears prickled David's eyes. He missed his Mother and Father so much. He could still smell the familiar scent of his Mother on her sheets. The pain was almost too much to bare.

His pain turned to anger as he tried to process what to do. He would make Eldon pay for what he had done to his parents. Eldon would wish to god that he had never messed with his family.

Thoughts of his parents mingled with ideas of how to punish Eldon. They swirled hypnotically in his mind. As David planned his revenge, his thoughts slowly fell away and sleep took him over.

The Chamber

'Help me check if they have a pulse!' Screamed Kaia. 'If any of them still have brain function, we can bring them back to life in the chamber that we have here on the ship.'

Isadora didn't know what Kaia meant, but she knew enough to know that she wanted them to check the fallen crew to see if they were still alive.

'Father still has a pulse!' Shouted Adama. 'Here help me get him over to the chamber!' He shouted.

Orion and Adama carried Tiamut over to what looked like a bench at the back of the ship. They laid him quickly down on the bench and Kaia went over and activated it with her mind. The bench began to glow a bright white light. Obviously something was happening but Isadora did not understand what.

As she bent down to check one of the crew members to see if they had a pulse, the realisation of what had just happened hit her. She hoped that she was wrong. But all the evidence pointed to General Myers being the one who had opened fire on the Valdons and slaughtered them in what could have been a peaceful takeover.

'Yes, yes its working!' Adama laughed and Isadora saw the colour begin to return into Adama's cheeks. She looked at Tiamut on the bed and he began to open his eyes.

'Ah Son, you managed to save me!' Smiled Tiamut and he put his hand on Adama's face.

Adama gasped a sigh of relief that stifled tears. 'Thank the creator, I thought that I'd lost you Father!'

'It will take more than a bullet from a surface human's weapon to finish me off Son.' Smiled Tiamut and whilst Adama smiled back he fretfully looked in Isadora's direction.

Isadora looked back down and carried on checking the casualties. Rala did not have a pulse. Isadora felt so sad there had to be something she could do. She went to check Centaurus. She heard Kaia's voice. 'It's too late Isadora, they are gone. We cannot save them. If they have some brain function, we are able to bring them back with the Technology that we have. But the fallen have been gone too long.' Kaia put her head in her hands and sobbed. 'We have failed them!'

'How did this happen? How did this happen?' Kaia shouted into the space ship in anguish. 'How did we lose our friends? Was the plan not clear? Hyperion, she exclaimed, my sweet Hyperion. I am so sorry that I failed you. I will meet you in the next life my friend.' Kaia whispered into Hyperion's chest as she sobbed.

'You didn't fail anyone,' said Adama leaving his Father to walk over to Kaia. 'It was all General Myers. Adama shook his head. I should have known that low life would pull a trick like this. He wasn't happy with Hyperion being in control of the ship. He didn't like taking orders from him. I guess he didn't like the idea of taking the Valdons peacefully either and he wanted to use his new soldiers, Adama sneered. As soon as we arrived at Delavia he commanded the Clones to shoot everyone on the ship. They all just open fired at everyone. Hyperion saved me. He dove in front of me and pinned me to the floor so they thought I was dead. When General Myers landed the ship on the ground and he instructed the Clones to go off and shoot the remaining live Valdons. I snook up on him and tried to take the gun that he had from him. And the rest you saw. We never had a chance. I would be dead too if it wasn't for Hyperion. He gave his life for me. And now I will never be able to thank him.' Adama crouched down on the floor of the ship with his head in his hands. 'I cannot believe what has just happened.'

Kaia stopped sobbing and wiped her face. 'We have to make sure that our friends have not died in vain here,' she said quietly. 'We have to make this count. Orion, can you go and check the situation with the Clones? I'm guessing that they will have shorted out when General Myers died as he was the one controlling them?'

'No need Ma-am they are neutralized.' Confirmed the ravishing Cowboy. 'They were linked in consciousness to General Myers. As soon as I put a bullet in his brain and his brain function shut down. He then released control of the Clones and they all shorted. We do not need to worry about them anymore.' Orion winked.

'What about the Valdons?' Asked Kaia weakly.

'None surviving by the looks of things!' Confirmed Orion.

'And Valdazar and the rest of the Valdon Army were blown up with the ship?' Kaia surmised.

'So it would seem Ma-am, agreed Orion. Has anyone seen our hairy, orange friend?' Asked the Cowboy.

'We need to go find Chinga!' Realised Isadora. 'He may need our help.'

'Yes,' agreed Kaia. 'We must find Chinga. Adama you stay on the ship with your Father as he regains his strength. Everybody else, follow me.'

And with that, the party from Earth stepped off the Agarthan ship and into the smoke filled air of Delavia.

The Next Morning

David was so nervous at breakfast. He hadn't slept much last night. He had spent a lot of the night crying for his parents. And the rest of the night imaging what it would be like when Peets and his army freed him. He really, really hoped that Peets was there today at the end of the exercise yard.

What if he wasn't there? Then he really was alone in this world. David swallowed the thought back down. No, he had faith. He had asked God for help yesterday as he didn't think that he could go on anymore and God had answered his prayers. He had brought him Peets. And Peets had access to a huge army of Bears and Cockroaches that hated the evil humans as much as he did. They were going to come and save them all.

He had forced himself to eat the lumpy porridge that had been provided for him at breakfast even though the greasy texture of it made him want to heave his little stomach up. You always had to make sure that you ate all of your food. As if you didn't, you could get sick. Mother and Father had always taught him that and he was not going to let them down now. He could not get sick, because he had to be the one to free his people. He looked around the breakfast area at all of the people. They looked scared and tired and hungry. Don't worry my friends he thought. My friend and I have a plan.

And we will free you all.

The Ancients

Orion had confirmed what Kaia had suspected and the Clones had all short circuited upon General Myers death. Isadora did not know why this was and she didn't want to ask as everybody else just seemed to accept it as normal.

All of the Clones therefore were laying on the floor motionless and all of the Valdons had been killed in the fight. Apart from one. Orion had not seen him as he was smaller than the rest and had managed to hide, obscured by one of the gargantuan Ancient Sasquatch. As soon as the Valdon had seen the party from Earth jump off the spaceship, it had literally run up to Orion, dropped to his knees and given himself up in fits of tears. Much to Orion's amusement. '*Hell I didn't even do anything and he's fallen at my feet!*'

They made their way through the piles of huge Valdon bodies and the smaller Clones, when suddenly Chinga broke through the trees running.

'My friends!' he shouted and ran over to them. Isadora ran to him and hugged him.

'Chinga! You're OK? I'm so glad!' Then Isadora realised that two more furry brown shapes were walking up behind him.

'Your family!' Shrieked Isadora! 'Ahhh I'm so happy that I finally get to meet them!'

'Yes!' Said Chinga smiling, but his face still looked sad. What was wrong?

The other adult Sasquatch behind Chinga started to speak. 'It's our Son Peets,' said Lamay. 'He went looking for Chinga as he was worried about him. He thought that if he went and fetched his Father then he could help take down the Valdons. He went through the portal to the Honey planet and he has not come back since.'

Orion and Chinga looked at each other in alarm. 'Chinga!' Said Orion for once looking worried. 'That portal stopped going to Earth not long after we went back through it. God knows where it is aligned to now? I closed it down for a while after we returned through it. But if he's managed to go through it, it won't have gone to Earth my friend!' Said Orion in panic.

'I know!' Said Chinga gravely. He stared at the floor. He turned to his mate. 'I will find him my love, but I might have to ask my Agarthan friends here for a bit more help. We Sasquatch have only ever known when the times are that the portal would take us to the Honey planet. We have never been interested in anything else. We have everything that we need and love here on Delavia. Why go anywhere else? The only reason we have gone to Earth over the years is to obtain more Honey for the people as there wasn't enough for us here. And I guess because we came from Earth we still have a connection to it. Do you Agarthans have the Technology to tell me where that portal will have taken my little boy to?' Chinga sounded like he was pleading for his life. He knew he had already asked too much of his new friends. And by the looks of all the bodies which lay on the floor in the rogue spaceship, his new friends had paid a high price.

Kaia smiled at the huge Sasquatch. 'Yes of course my friend. We will be able to look at the times and give you some options as to where he will probably have gone. Do not worry, we will find him. We promised you that we would help you get back your family. And that means all of your family. We will continue to help you until you have found your Son.' She reassured.

Chinga broke down in tears. 'Thank you so much Kaia, my family and I are eternally grateful to you. I am so so sorry for all you have lost here today. I feel like this is my fault. Without me asking for help you would not be here. Yet still even after all that. Even after what you have personally lost here today. You offer your help to me again in my time of need even though you have yourself lost so much. I feel so humbled. Thank you so very much.'

Kaia smiled a sad smile. 'We will always offer help to those who deserve it my friend. It is not your fault what happened here today. I take responsibility for this myself. I knew General Myers was unstable. I knew he was blood thirsty. And I knew he wanted a war. And I let him go with Hyperion. I should have kept him on my ship where I could have monitored the situation more closely. Instead I put him with Hyperion as I thought he would respond better to being directed by a Male. This is my responsibility to bear. And I need to make amends for what has happened here. I am so sorry Chinga for the devastation that has been caused to your beautiful planet,' said Kaia as she surveyed the scorched and smouldering landscape.

'But you have my word, we will find your Son.'

Break Time

As David lined up to wait for the huge steel doors to open to let him outside, his little chest heaved. He could feel a trickle of sweat dripping down his back. He felt a bit dizzy. No do not pass out now. Not today. Peets is waiting. He started breathing long slow deep breaths and slowly the world stopped spinning. The high pitched horn sounded signalling that break time had started and the steel doors started to open. He had never felt so alive. He wanted to run. Literally run across the yard to the back and scream 'Peets are you here?' But he knew that he did not want to draw attention to himself. He slowly began his walk across the huge yard. He tried not to walk in a straight line but zig zag a bit to make it look like he really didn't know where his legs were going to take him. But in his mind's eye his attention was solely focussed on the place where he had met Peets yesterday. As he walked across the yard, he kept momentarily looking up to see if he could see his furry friend. Yes, he was sure he could see what looked like fur! Peets was there, he was really there! He had come back like he said he would!

Suddenly a large shape stepped in front of him obscuring the light. He looked up before he walked into it. Oh no! No! Not today, please no. He swallowed down fear and apprehension whilst adrenaline spiked in his body.

It was Nathan. Nathan was an older boy than David. And he was a bully. He got off on taking his frustrations out on the smaller kids, and it looked like today it was David's turn. Nathan's Father was one of the informants within the population. Everyone knew it. He was 'in' with the guards. He passed on information about people for 'privileges'. In other words Nathans Father was a snitch. Nathans Father was scum.

'Where are your parents, skinny rat?' Nathan said in a low, menacing voice.

David swallowed, his eyes darted to where he knew Peets was laying.

'They took them, they took them three nights ago.' David said in a low voice trying not to let his voice crack. But talking about his parents was too hard for him, it was all so raw and fresh.

'Ah looks like the little baby is going to cry!' Nathan said gleefully to his two friends that he always had stuck to his side. 'Well your stupid parents must have been doing something wrong if they took them skinny rat. At least that's what Father always says,' Nathan smirked.

Anger swelled inside David's tiny tummy. It made his guts hurt and his eyes started to swim with angry tears.

'Only babies cry,' sneered Nathan happily as he watched the emotion in David's face. 'It looks like we're going to have to teach you a lesson!' Nathan jumped towards David and began hitting him.

As the lights started to go out and everything swirled to black. As he could hear the two thug friends of Nathan laughing and cheering him on. All David could think of is 'Please! Don't let Peets leave!'

'Please don't let him leave me! We have to break out! I have to get home!'

Then nothing.

Honey

Isadora finally stood in front of the Ancients. The whole reason why she had initially been brought here a few days ago. Kaia had managed to make their huge cages vanish. Isadora had no idea how Kaia had done this and when she had looked at Kaia to ask. Kaia had just laughed and said 'magic'.

Isadora looked up at the Ancients and began to speak with them telepathically. 'My name is Isadora Stone. I come from Earth which is known by your kind as the Honey planet. I am a friend of Chinga. I met him in the woods at the back of my house one night when I was star gazing. I was eating Honey sandwiches and the smell drew him out I guess. We have been friends ever since. Chinga comes to our planet for Honey. He tells me he comes as your people love Honey and that the Honey that you have here on Delavia, is not shared out fairly amongst the people. Because of this, your people come to our planet to obtain our Honey. But there is a big problem with that. The Honey on Earth is starting to get contaminated. It is starting to not be healthy to eat any more. The reason for this is because humans do not look after the planet. The oceans are full of our plastic. The air is full of our chemicals and metals. The ground is full of pesticides to make things grow quicker. A sickness is taking over the Earth and it is because of us humans and how we live. It is effecting the plants and the pollen and nectar that they produce. The pollen is full of chemicals, and pesticides and this is poisoning the Honey. It is because of our Honey that your people have become sick. And for that I must apologise. On behalf of humanity. As our carelessness and lack of respect for our environment and Mother Earth has now affected you on your planet and impacted on your kind too. I intend to speak to someone really high up about this when I get back. In fact, I am going to try my best to speak to The President about this as I think if we don't do something about this soon, there will be no Earth left to save. So I apologise. I apologise that our Honey has made you sick. But I ask of you, now that you know that your kind cannot eat our Honey as it is poison to them. Please can you share the Honey that you do have on Delavia amongst your people? I don't want to see any more of your people get sick and die because of the inconsideration of *my* people.'

The Ancients had been listening to this brave young women in grave silence. They felt terrible. They had been so selfish. How could they have done this to their own people? They would never be able to right the wrongs that they had inflicted on their own people. But they would try. And they would start now.

The Ancients began to speak telepathically back to Isadora and their huge voices boomed in Isadora's head.

'It is we who are ashamed brave girl. We should never have been so selfish. We should never have been so greedy. We caused this harm amongst our people. And it is we who will fix the situation. From now on the Honey of Delavia will be shared amongst all of the people, equally. You have our word.'

Chinga, Lamay and Sneets screamed and hugged each other jumping up and down. They must tell the people. Where were they? Chinga thought.

Sneets explained to him that the rest of their people were hiding out in the caves and had offered to go and tell them that it was now safe to come out. Chinga and Lamay said they would go with her so she wouldn't be alone. It was also decided in that moment that when they got back, Chinga and his family would travel back to Earth and into the Agartha City once more, in the rogue ship piloted by Adama and Tiamut. Once at Agartha City, Kaia and Orion would help Chinga work out where Peets had gone through the portal. Isadora was to be dropped back off at home in Kaia's ship and Orion would come with them. 'I picked you up from your school Miss Isadora, I wanna make sure you get back home safe now.'

Kaia also explained, much to the happiness of the huge Ancients. That in order to heal their people who had become sick, they would find their cure in the Honey produced on Delavia. The pureness of the Delavian Honey would undo all the damage that the Earth Honey had created. And it would heal the sick. Chinga would have been very excited indeed to think that he could eat as much Delavian Honey as he wanted, if he hadn't have had the worry of where his little boy was. All he could think about was Peets and where he had gone. But he would find him. He knew he would.

There was just one more loose end to tie up. They all looked at the remaining Valdon who had been on his knees witnessing everything that had just happened and intermittently snivelling.

What did they do with him?

As they stared at the snivelling Valdon they noticed a blinking light on his chest. It was some form of camera. 'I'll take care of that my friend' said Orion and he punched the Valdon square in the chest where the blinking light was. The light flickered and disappeared. Smoke streamed out of its chest.

The Valdon burst into fresh tears.

The End

'Bring me the thing!' Valdazar screamed in fury, hopping around in anger. He was seething. How DARE they! Nobody beat him! NOBODY! I am Valdazar!

'Ah, what thing Sire?' The huge Valdon in front of Valdazar's throne said meekly. He knew that he would be on the receiving end of his Masters rage.

'The thing, the thing, that THING! That I see things through!' Screamed Valdazar. He was so mad he couldn't even think properly. 'I just threw it on the floor! Get it for me now!'

'You mean your Smart Glass Pad Sire.' Human whispered from behind the shadows of Valdazar's throne.

'I don't care what it's called Human. Just fetch it for me, now!'

A large Valdon lumbered to where the clear piece of Perspex was resting on the floor and brought it back to his master. It was so tiny in comparison to the Valdons hand it was like carrying a postage stamp.

Valdazar snatched it from the creature's hand. The Valdon jumped back like it had been shot.

Valdazar tried to connect with any of his Valdons on Delavia. Surely there must be some of them alive still? The piece of Technology molded to his hand and began shimmering. The camera clicked on, on his one remaining Valdons chest. Gradually the current scene that was happening on Delavia shimmered on the piece of Technology. The stupid, fat Ancients were stood there having a conversation with, a girl? Some young blonde girl?

'Who is this girl?' Valdazar sneered. 'And why is she the one speaking to those fat, disgusting creatures?'

Human from behind Valdazar's throne. Where he always was, watching and waiting for his master's next command, casually glanced at the Smart Glass Pad on his Masters Hand.

I wonder who Valdazar's next conquest will be, Human thought sadly. Human looked at the pretty blonde girl currently speaking telepathically with the Ancients.

Time stood still.

No! White noise rushed into Human's ears.

NO! NO! NO! He could not believe his eyes.

Human fell to his knees behind his Masters throne.

How could this be? He asked himself as the world began spinning.

Isadora?

How had she found him?

'Who is this girl?' Spat Valdazar as he threw the contraption again in sheer rage and it pinged off the floor, narrowly missing slicing the jugular of another Valdon.

*It's my daughter.......*thought Human. In sheer panic.

'FIND HER!' Shouted Valdazar in white hot fury, 'and bring her to me at once! How dare she think she can overthrow me? I am Valdazar! He raged, and how old is she for god's sake? About 14?'

She's 15, just turned thought Human sadly as tears leaked down his face and sadness and happiness burst from his chest all at the same time. The only thing that had kept him going was the thought that one day he might see his daughter again.

Humans mind was racing. His head was spinning. He quickly picked himself up off the floor and wiped his eyes before his Master directed his murderous gaze to him.

Is it really Isadora?

Is it really my Izzy?

Is she looking for me?

Hope and fear filled his chest and he struggled to breathe.

Oh my god he wants her.

She can't be hurt.

I must protect her. I *must* keep her as far away from this evil madman as possible.

What can I do?

Humans mind flicked back to the day he was taken and the last time that he had seen his daughter. He had replayed that image over and over in his head whilst he had been a captive of Valdazar. She had looked older in her face than when he had last seen her. But that was my Izzy he thought.

It had been a normal Saturday afternoon. The day that it had happened.

Isadora and Mrs Stone were making brownies in the kitchen for them to eat after tea. He was going to Walmart to pick up something for tea. He'd got in the car and was travelling down the dirt track at the back of their house which leads to the main road. It was broad daylight. One minute he was in the car, and the next there was a blinding flash of light and his surroundings had changed. At first he thought he had been in a crash. But when he opened his eyes and saw the two large, ugly giants in front of him. He knew that this was no crash.

The next few days and weeks had been a blur. They had taken him as they knew he was a telepath. Human had always been careful to keep this part of himself hidden. Even from his family. But the Valdons had Technology which could sense this higher level of consciousness. They had been specifically looking for someone just like him. And a couple of rogue scout Valdons had just stumbled upon him whilst they were scanning new lands for their master. It could have been anyone that they had taken. But he guessed that there weren't many humans on Earth who were telepathic. They had drugged him and gradually broken his mind until he had no more fight left in him. No more desire to escape. Only fear of his Master.

He spent most of his days trying to avoid the scrutiny of Valdazar. But over time he had turned into his Masters greatest asset as he could communicate with all life forms in the Universe. And Valdazar came in contact with most of them. They spent every day flying from planet to planet, conquering, overthrowing and then bartering with other scum that roamed space to swap what they had acquired for new Technology. His master was obsessed with Technology and having the best of everything. And he was ruthless. Human had seen him kill thousands of beings all over the Universe, just to access the newest piece of Technology or spaceship. And now he was after his daughter.

My Izzy.

Human could not let that happen.

Home

The journey back home was bitter sweet for Isadora. Sweet as she got to see her Momma. She had missed her so very much. Bitter as she had had to say goodbye to Chinga and who knew how often she would get to see him, now that he would no longer be coming to Earth to eat our Honey. He would be happy though as he now could eat as much of the Delavian Honey as he wanted. She really, really hoped that they would be able to find his little boy. But she was confident that if anyone could find him Kaia and Orion could. And that made her happy. She bet that Peets was so scared wherever he was. But she knew that if he was anything like his Father, he would make it back to Delavia. Her thoughts momentarily flicked to her Father and she felt tears glisten in her eyes. If only Daddy were at home too.

She had also had to say goodbye to Adama too. They had awkwardly hugged and said it had been nice to meet each other. With Tiamut being recently injured, she understood that Adama had not wanted to upset his Father. She also knew what Tiamut's wishes were. And she respected them. It never would have gone anywhere anyway. She was 15 years old, how was she supposed to date someone who lived underneath the ground? It was hard enough to meet up with a boy who just lived down your street without a car.

Well Adama did have a spaceship she laughed inside.

The spaceship stopped.

'We're here Isadora!' Orion shouted.

'Now you take care of yourself do you hear?' The gorgeous Cowboy drawled at Isadora as he kissed her hand. 'The next time I see you I don't want you telling me stories of how you let those girls at your school upset you. You are worth a million of them all combined together and then some Isadora do you hear?'

Isadora smiled slowly and blinked. 'The next time you see me? There'll be a next time Orion?'

'Oh yes Isadora, there's always a next time.' The handsome alien drawled and he gestured to the door which was opening on the craft.

'Bye Kaia,' Isadora said hugging the beautiful blond haired priestess. 'I hope I get to see you again sometime?'

'You will Isadora. And don't forget, I can always contact you telepathically to fill you in on what is happening with Chinga's family. BUT make sure that you practice on that shield of white light. That way you can protect your thoughts and only let in who you want to come in.' Kaia smiled.

'Don't go givin her ideas now,' drawled Orion. 'I like listened to what she's thinking. Especially the parts about me!' Orion winked.

Isadora smiled

'I will work on my shield Kaia I promise. But I would love to hear from you. I really want to know that they find Peets and that he will be OK?'

'Don't you worry about that now Isadora, old Orion's got it under control.' The gorgeous Cowboy tipped his hat.

Isadora gave one last smile to both Orion and Kaia and started walking towards the door on the craft. The next minute she was stood in front of her own front door. How on Earth had that happened? They must have given me a boost somehow. She had seen so many weird and wonderful things over the last few days, she shouldn't find that strange at all she thought.

A bubble of excitement ran up her spine as she thought about seeing her Momma. She turned back round to wave off the craft, only to find that the craft had already disappeared.

She was suddenly aware of how cold the night was.

She opened the door as quickly as she was able.

'Momma, I'm back!' Isadora shouted.

Mrs Stone ran into the kitchen.

'Oh thank goodness you are OK Isadora. I must admit I was considering starting to get a little bit worried. You've been gone ages and I haven't heard a thing. What about the email you were going to send me?'

Isadora laughed inside. If only her Momma knew what had really been happening to her daughter. Did they have internet access on the Moon? They probably did Isadora thought.

'Sorry Momma, I was having so much fun I just forgot!'

Mrs Stone was just about to carry on chastising her daughter when the phone rang.

'Who's that calling at this time of night?' Mrs Stone muttered, angry that her reunion with her daughter had been interrupted.

'Hello,' said Mrs Stone sharply.

The voice of The President of the United States cascaded down the line and into Mrs Stone's ears.

'Mrs Stone? It's the President of the United States here. I'm calling you about your daughter Isadora.'

Mrs Stone looked incredulously at Isadora and back at the phone.

'Ah hello Mr President Sir. Yes this is Mrs Stone.'

'I wonder if I might trouble you for the company of your daughter tomorrow if you don't have anything previously planned? I could send a car for her around 9am?' The President purred down the phone.

'Er, certainly Mr President. That's fine Sir.' Mrs Stone said baffled.

'Excellent Mrs Stone. Tell Isadora I will see her tomorrow. Goodnight!'

'Goodnight Sir!'

Mrs Stone replaced the receiver slowly on the phone and stared at her daughter.

'That was the President of the United States on the phone Isadora. He says he's picking you up at 9am tomorrow morning in a car. What kind of Geography trip was this that you were on?' Mrs Stone said in amazement.

Isadora laughed. Good news travels fast hey? How did he know I wanted to see him? Isadora thought quizzically

So many crazy things had happened over the last few days. Why should it seem strange that The President wants to speak with me?

Maybe he can hear my thoughts too? Everybody else can!

Isadora laughed so hard Mrs Stone thought she was losing her mind.

Just in case

The soldier reported on the other end of the phone.

'There has been some 'activity' Sir. Which could potentially have some repercussions for Earth. Some big repercussions. We may come under attack very soon.'

There was silence on the other end of the phone.

'Sir?' The soldier checked that he was being heard.

'Yes I heard you'. More silence. 'OK,.........put the barrier up.' The voice said.

'The main barrier Sir? Around Earth?' The soldier checked.

'Yes the main barrier around Earth.' The voice said impatiently.

'Yes, that's what I said.'

'Ahhh, Sir. This will stop anyone being able to leave the Earth or enter the Earth's atmosphere. At all Sir.' The soldier checked.

'Yes I am fully aware of that.' Said the voice. 'Do it.'

'Yes Sir.' The soldier replied and cancelled the call.

No-one will be attacking Earth, whispered the voice.

THE END (*For now*)

Thank you so very much my friends!

Thank you so much for reading my Debut Novel 'Isadora Stone and the Magic Portal!'
To find out what happens to Isadora, Adama, Peets, David and all of Isadora's new friends. Please look out for **'Isadora Stone and the Battle for Inner Earth'** which will be out in print and kindle edition in October 2019.

If you enjoyed my book, please do tell a friend!

Many thanks for reading

Love and Light to you all

Laura Anne Whitworth

Made in the USA
Coppell, TX
21 January 2024

27953745R00142